©

ISBN 9781093991178

First Printing Edition 2019

Plush Publishing
P.O. Box 851313
Westland, Michigan 48185
www.plushpublishing.com

Acknowledgements

First, I want to thank God for being better to me, than I have been to myself. Without Him, I am nothing. He has given me strength when I was weak, peace in the middle of my storms, vision when I was lost, and hope when I felt like I couldn't go on. His grace and mercy is everlasting.

To my father and mother, my guardian angels! Every day without you here on earth with me is hard. I thank you for all the sacrifices you made, that molded me into the woman I am today. I thank you for all the wisdom, morals and structure you instilled into me. Even when you thought I wasn't listening, I WAS LISTENING! Not one day goes by that I don't thank God for giving me two of the best parents in the world. You were supposed to be here to see this, but I know you are here with me in spirit. I love you and I pray I am making you proud. Keep watching over me and your grandbabies.

To my children; my hearts, my loves, you are my daily inspiration. When I have thought of giving up, I had to remember who was watching, YOU! I have made some mistakes in front of you, I pray it has taught you, to let your mistakes BUILD YOU, not BREAK YOU! Your love and loyalty have gotten me through some of my worst days. I thank you for sitting on that front row EVERY last one of my court dates, I thank you for being the first face I saw out of surgery from being shot. If nobody got me, I know my kids DO! I could not have asked God to bless with me with better kids.

To my daughter India. You inspire my heart! You have taught me to chase my dreams and never give up. I am OVER proud of the woman you are growing into daily.

Special thank you to my daughter Lea Haislip AKA Akeelah the Bee LOL for editing my work and catching all my mistakes

To my brothers! Thank you for being some of the last REAL ones left. Last of a dying breed!

To my best friends Brandy, Kerry, and Valencia, and my sisters Felicia and Porscha; I thank you for always being my listening ear and never judging me. I thank you for your brutal, unfiltered, no sugar coating, honesty (I think, lol). You have never held back, always telling me what I needed to hear instead of what I wanted to hear. Every woman needs a supportive circle. I thank God for mine.

To all my supporters, Thank You! Thank You! Thank YOU! I Love You! Without you there is no me.
To EVERY Woman reading this. If it's ONE message I hope this book sends to each and every last one of you it is: no matter how bad your situation looks, NEVER GIVE UP. GOD IS ALWAYS IN CONTROL!
The Devil comes to kill, steal and destroy! He will do everything in his power to kill your joy, steal your peace, and destroy your hope. You will be tested, whatever you do DON'T FOLD!
To all my haters, betrayers, and everyone who counted me out; I guess no one told you I was a seed.
Every piece of dirt you threw on me, I used to help me grow. I thank you for all the lies, ridicule, and betrayals in hopes of ruining me. It made me stronger, wiser and richer!
If I have encouraged or inspired just ONE WOMAN, it was all worth it!

Domestic violence comes in all shapes, and forms! Just because you are not being physically assaulted does not mean you aren't being abused. Name calling, intimidation, forced sex acts, embarrassment, ridicule, constant false accusations, and alienating you from your family and friends are ALL forms of abuse. The abuser may change TEMPORARILY, but it won't last long! Asking God for a sign IS A SIGN! They won't change! Get out before it's too late!

He Played Me

Synopsis

Have you ever had a flashback over your entire life and thought about every horrible decision you have ever made? How different your life could have been if only you had made the right decisions? This is a story of how lust, love, lies, and sex can lead you down a dark path full of passion, jealousy, hate, betrayals, and ultimately your demise.

Yazmin has been in a sexless, loveless marriage for the past two years. She is content but not happy. That is until the charming and powerful Jai comes strolling into her life. He is everything she desires in a man; charming, handsome, with just the right amount of street swag. But everything that glitters isn't gold! And sometimes the grass looks greener on the other side because it's fake!

Nadia has been in an abusive marriage for the past ten years. She has enjoyed a lavish life of fancy cars, exotic trips, diamonds and furs, but not without enduring the countless black eyes, outside kids, and being pimped out by her husband, that has come along with it. What would it take for her to realize nothing her husband ever gave her was more valuable than her life?

Jai is charming, controlling, and manipulative. He uses his power and money to control and mistreat every woman in his life. He sees women as nothing more than trophies, used to boast his ego. That is, until he meets the beautiful and sexy Yazmin.

When their three worlds collide, they will learn one of life's hardest lessons! Betrayal wouldn't be betrayal, if it didn't come from someone you love!

Prologue

I Tell All My Niggas Cut the Check
Buss It Down, turn your goofy down pound
I'mma do splits on it, yes, splits on it
I'm a bad bitch I'mma throw fits on it
I'mma bust it open, I'mma go stupid and be
a ditz on it
I don't date honey, cookie on tsunami
All my niggas wife me once they get that
good punani

The Detroit summer anthem *Rake It Up* by Yo Gotti pumped through Yazmin's car speakers. Yazmin was feeling like a bad bitch as she turned into her Southfield condominium rapping along to her favorite song. As the music thumped through her car speakers, she rapped along with Nikki Minaj, pulling into the parking lot. Enjoying her slight buzz from the few Hennessy and Cokes she had just consumed at the social club she owned, Yazmin grabbed her purse and phone to make it in the house before the rain started to come down too hard. It was a beautiful night out for it to be mid-October, but that's Michigan for you, she thought. Just like these niggas, you never know what the fuck to expect! As Yazmin approached her front door an uneasy feeling overcame her body, giving her goosebumps. She looked around and only saw what appeared to be a disabled man scurrying to get out of the rain, he glanced back at her, smiled and continued his way. Yazmin wondered if he received disability checks, *Rake It Up, Rake It Up* she hummed and laughed to herself. She wasn't always a cold-hearted bitch, but after being in an abusive marriage for years, followed by the ultimate act of betrayal by her most recent ex-husband she was now an emotionless bitch when it came to men. Just as she put her key in the door, a shot rang out and she instantly felt a terrible burning sensation in her leg. As she looked back, Yazmin could only get a glimpse of the man she assumed was disabled a few seconds ago, holding a gun before the flash from the muzzle momentarily blinded her. Her flight or fight instincts kicked in instantly and she turned her key to get into the house. If she could just make it inside, her gun was right within arm's reach of the door. *"Fuck!"* she thought. Out of all the times to not have her gun on her! Just as she got the door open, she felt another bullet rip through her flesh. Yazmin dove in the house and kicked the door shut as bullet after bullet was shot through the door. Once she felt the third bullet pierce her body and heard the gunman on the other side of the door reloading the gun, she knew this was it. As Yazmin looked down and saw the blood pouring from her wounds, she couldn't believe her own karma had finally caught up with her. *Damn, my kids,* were her last thought before everything went black.

Chapter 1

As Terry pumped in and out of her, Yazmin laid there looking up at the ceiling wondering what she would make with the chicken she took out the freezer last night; maybe smothered chicken and wild rice, she thought. Suddenly, Terry stopped his pitiful strokes and looked down at her. "What's wrong baby?" Terry asked. "Am I not hitting it right?" What Yazmin wanted to tell him was, he had never once hit it right, instead she nibbled on his bottom lip the way he liked and reassured him he was pleasing her. Yazmin began to kiss her husband's neck, as she tried to slyly slide from underneath him and get in her favorite position, on all fours with her plump ass in the air. But before she could fully twist her body into position, Terry stopped her. "Baby you know I don't believe in all that freak in the sheets bullshit, I want my wife old fashioned at all times, even in the bedroom!" he flatly said. As Terry laid her back down and slowly eased his thick dick back into her, Yazmin started back with her rehearsed moans. She matched every amateur thrust he delivered with a sexy moan, followed by a "Yes baby, right there!" while she went back to contemplating their dinner menu for tonight. Fuck it, he would be done in less than five minutes, Yazmin thought, maybe sooner if she threw it back. As soon as Terry fell asleep, Yazmin pulled out her newest toy, a ten-inch chocolate toy, "The Pussy Pleaser," and brought herself to a mind-blowing orgasm, just like she had done damn near every night for the past two years of her marriage.

As Yazmin padded through the house getting ready for work, she enjoyed the feel of the plush white carpet under her toes. She loved her beautiful, four bedroom, three thousand square foot home Terry had built from the ground up in a quiet, gated suburban area, as a wedding present to her. Yazmin couldn't deny her husband was an excellent provider, who took great care of her, well financially; it was the emotional and sexual satisfaction that was seriously lacking in their marriage. It didn't help that Terry was a severe functional alcoholic, with old fashioned views on just about everything. If Yazmin were to be truthful, she knew her and Terry were not compatible from the start. Being that they both came from two-family households, with parents who had been married for over forty years, they shared similar morals, values and beliefs. Yazmin took great pride in her job as a bank teller, where she has been employed for the past ten years. While Terry was rapidly climbing the ladder with one of the top distributing companies within the state. However, the similarities stopped there. While Yazmin was a confident and outgoing person, Terry was shy and awkward. Yazmin believed in open communication and Terry barely talked at all. Yazmin had a high sex drive and loved to experiment in the bedroom; she felt nothing should be off limits with two people in a committed relationship. She blushed as she thought about her husband's beautiful, chocolate, nine-inch dick, with its nice smooth round head, that he had no damn idea how to use, and even worse refused to learn. Yazmin had tried everything from slipping pornos in the DVD, to "accidently" dropping her list of bedroom fantasies in his car. Unfortunately, all her efforts had gotten her nothing more than a drunkard lecture on "lady-like" bedroom behavior and countless nights of boring, unsatisfying missionary sex, that left her pussy desperate for some good dick attention. Some might think she was a selfish dumb bitch for even worrying about sexual and emotional satisfaction when she has a husband with a good job, good credit and that comes home every night to her, and after losing her home, her job, her reputation and damn near her life, they just might be right.

Chapter 2

"Next in line," Yazmin called out as she checked the time on her watch to see how much longer until her lunch break. Yazmin cherished her job, but the day after day stress of dealing with customers who constantly took their frustrations out on her was beginning to take a toll on her. Every time she would try to talk to Terry about starting her own business, at least online for now, she would get the "women aren't meant to be entrepreneurs" lecture. Little did Terry know; she had already started investing into her own business and would be launching her website very soon. Yazmin came from a family of entrepreneurs and hustlers and while she was thankful for her job, she always desired more. As her next customer approached her window, Yazmin groaned under her breath when she realized who it was, Nadia, the customer from hell! How did she always get the same loud mouth, ghetto bitch every time she came into the office? "How may I help you today ma'am?" Yazmin asked, in the most professional voice she could muster up. "I need to make a withdrawal from my account!" Nadia snobbishly said as she threw her items on the counter, just missing hitting Yazmin with them. Yazmin silently counted to ten in her head, before responding. "I'll be right back; a manager has to sign for a withdrawal this big!" As she turned to walk away, she could feel Nadia's eyes on her. Yazmin returned and placed the bills on the money counter, while Nadia awkwardly stared at her. *What the fuck is this bitch's problem?* Yazmin thought to herself. She hurried to finish the transaction before she said something that would cause her to lose her job. As Nadia walked away, Yazmin couldn't help but to notice how huge her ass was. What she lacked in the face, she definitely made up for in the ass, she laughed. Nadia turned back and caught Yazmin staring at her ass, winked, and licked her plump lips. When she felt the moisture between her legs, Yazmin knew right then and there, Nadia would be trouble. She just didn't know how much trouble she would really be.

The remainder of Yazmin's day flew by and before she knew it, it was closing time. As she finished up her last customer of the day, she was thankful the day was over. She had plans to go by the mall and pick up a few housewarming items for her oldest son, Desmond, who had just moved into his first apartment. Yazmin was very proud of both of her sons; at the ages of twenty and eighteen, they both had graduated high school, had valid driver licenses, enrolled in college and had never been arrested a day in their lives. Those were all rarities for a young black man growing up in the gritty city of Detroit. Yazmin loved her children and tried to keep hold of them as tight as possible, but as they developed into their manhood every day, she had to accept they had their own lives. Although she was sad when Desmond announced he would be moving out, Yazmin was proud of him for taking the first step into adulthood. Yazmin stepped into her manager's office to drop her daily deposit into the office safe. Her manager, Megan, was sitting behind her desk humming a beautiful melody, just as excited as everyone else to be leaving work for the day. "Yes, honey it's Friday!" Megan sang in her heavy accent. Megan was a beautiful chocolate woman, with gorgeous smooth skin, thick Jamaican curves, and the prettiest accent Yazmin had ever heard. Yazmin was always amazed at how Megan could easily turn her accent on and off. When Megan interacted with customers, she used a polished, professional voice with little, to no trace, of an accent at all, however when Megan was happy or excited her accent was undeniable. Yazmin loved having Megan as a manager, she wasn't one of those managers who went out of their way to make their employee's lives miserable; if you came to work and did your job, she didn't bother you. Both ladies grabbed their jackets, said their goodbyes and were on their way to get their weekend started.

Chapter 3

As Yazmin struggled to carry her shopping bags out the mall, she laughed and shook her head at herself. What was only supposed to be a quick trip to the mall picking up a few items for her son's apartment, had turned into a mini shopping spree. Yazmin had purchased items for herself and her husband as well. Terry's birthday was coming up and he was in desperate need of a new wardrobe. While Yazmin prided herself on being fashionable, Terry felt buying new clothes before the old ones virtually had holes in them was just a waste of money. Yazmin's clothing consumed most of their huge walk-in closet. The only new clothes Terry owned, were the ones Yazmin purchased for him because she refused to step out with her husband looking like her hired help. As Yazmin stuffed the bags into the trunk of her Dodge Charger she decided to swing by the local bar for a quick drink and bite to eat instead of going home to be alone. Terry worked the afternoon shift and often picked up extra hours, so he was hardly ever home. Yazmin pulled into the bar's parking lot and freshened up her makeup before going in. At the age of thirty-nine, Yazmin still had a youthful look about herself. People often mistook her sons for her boyfriend when they went out together. At 5'1" and one hundred and fifty pounds, Yazmin could easily be described as a "bad bitch," with her beautiful pecan colored skin, nice 36DD breast, thick thighs, firm round ass, and a smile that could light up a room. The 22 inches of bone straight Brazilian hair she always wore added to her sex appeal. Yazmin was sexy and she knew it. As she entered the bar, Yazmin scanned the area to find an available seat. Just as she was about to sit down, she noticed Nadia sitting alone in a corner booth nursing a drink. She turned to head in the opposite direction, but Nadia looked up and they made eye contact, before she could. Yazmin could see Nadia had been crying, and while a part of her wanted to pretend she didn't recognize her, Yazmin just couldn't do it. She walked over to Nadia and asked her was she okay. Nadia began to sob so hard, Yazmin sat down next to her, rubbing her back, until the sobbing turned into hiccups. Yazmin and Nadia couldn't help but to giggle at how ridiculous Nadia sounded. Yazmin flagged a waitress over and ordered a bottle of champagne. She knew it was going to be a long night.

Over the next two hours, Yazmin and Nadia talked like old girlfriends. Yazmin was amazed at how much they had in common. They both loved fashion and urban fiction books, adored their sons, and both women were in unhappy marriages. Nadia's husband Dre stayed in and out of prison and was currently on his way home from a five-year prison bid. Yazmin was surprised to hear this information and wondered who the husky, good looking man Nadia often came into her job with. Yazmin didn't have to wonder for too long. By their second bottle of Champagne Yazmin learned the man was Nadia's side nigga Roy, her best friend's cousin, that she fell in love with over the last three years. Now that her husband was headed home from prison, Nadia had to decide on who she would be with. While Roy was fully aware of the situation, he refused to share Nadia with her husband once he was released from prison. Roy knew Nadia was married but it didn't bother him because he was the one pounding in her warmness every night, and he planned on keeping it that way. Roy gave Nadia an ultimatum, her husband or him. While Nadia did love her husband, she wasn't in love with him anymore. All the years of lying, cheating, abuse, and the fact that Dre had been in and out of prison most of their marriage had finally started to take a toll on her. At the age of forty-three, Nadia just wanted to be happy. As she sat across the table from Yazmin, she admired how her skin glowed. Deep down, Nadia hated Dre for taking that glow away from her. After receiving countless black eyes, busted lips, and even a fractured jaw at the hands of her husband, Nadia was now just a shell of the person she once was. Roy was a breath of fresh air for Nadia. He was smart, funny, intelligent, and treated Nadia like a lady. Although they never declared themselves in a relationship because of Nadia's situation, whatever Roy did in the streets never came back to her and she respected him for that. Nadia knew she deserved better then Dre, but for some reason she couldn't let him go. She prayed for God to send something to break the hold Dre had on her and little did she know that reason was sitting right in front of her.

Chapter 4

Yazmin and Nadia both had a nice smooth buzz when they finally left the bar, and neither were ready for the night to end. They decided to catch the latest Tyler Perry movie because they needed a good laugh. Yazmin was anxious to see the new theater that had just opened right down the street everyone was talking about. Yazmin and Terry were supposed to check the theater out weeks ago, but Terry always changed his mind about going at the last minute. After both ladies grabbed a few snacks from the concession stand, they got cozy in the reclining chairs and waited for the movie to start. Yazmin couldn't believe how empty the theater was for a Friday night. Besides her and Nadia, there was only one more couple in the entire theater. Yazmin guessed everyone was out enjoying the beautiful weather. Yazmin now regretted getting the dry popcorn as she watched Nadia dip her nachos in the creamy cheese. Just as Nadia placed a nacho in her mouth a string of cheese drizzled down her lips. Yazmin became instantly aroused watching Nadia lick it off. Yazmin had not noticed until just then how full and juicy Nadia's lips were. When Nadia looked over at Yazmin she smiled, dipped her finger in the cheese and placed it in Nadia's mouth. Yazmin swirled her tongue around Nadia's finger as she licked off the cheese. Yazmin wasn't sure if it was the champagne, lack of sex, or both that had her so horny. As Nadia leaned in to kiss her, she didn't try to stop her. Nadia eased her hand up Yazmin's dress and was happy to find she wasn't wearing any panties. Yazmin never did; her husband hated that. When Nadia started to massage Yazmin's clit, she softly moaned. Nadia reclined Yazmin's chair all the way back and climbed on top of her. As Nadia trailed kisses down Yazmin's body, she continued to massage her clit until her tongue replaced her fingers. Yazmin had never felt anything so good in her life. Nadia gently lifted Yazmin's legs and placed them on her shoulder, giving her full access to Yazmin sweetness. Nadia alternated from slowly licking her clit, to dipping her tongue in and out her ass. Yazmin had never had her ass eaten before; now she understood what all the hype was about, it felt great. As she felt her first orgasm approaching, she spread her legs further and held Nadia's head in place. Yazmin had to bite down on her lip to keep from screaming out in the theater as the most powerful orgasm she ever experienced took over her body. Yazmin tried to push Nadia away, but she had a firm grip on Yazmin's hips. As Yazmin looked down at her juices covering Nadia's full lips another orgasm took over her body. For the rest of the movie Nadia stayed on her knees with Yazmin's goodies in her mouth. Yazmin now knew why Roy was willing to be Nadia's side nigga for so many years; with how good Nadia worked her tongue, she was willing to be Nadia's side bitch as well.

Chapter 5

Nadia and Yazmin became inseparable over the next few months. They enjoyed lunch dates, shopping, taking trips together and a lot of great sex. Terry was so happy Yazmin was no longer nagging him about taking her places, he didn't mind how much time Yazmin was spending with her new found "friend." Yazmin couldn't remember the last time she felt the need to bring out any of her "little toys." Nadia's tongue was all she needed. Nadia and Yazmin decided to take a weekend trip to Miami for some down time. They both had very busy weeks coming up. Yazmin's grand opening for her boutique was in two weeks and Nadia's husband was due to be home any day. Nadia had booked the ladies a beautiful five-star suite with a huge balcony that overlooked the ocean. Once they checked their bags in, the ladies couldn't wait to get out and sightsee and do some shopping. Nadia and Yazmin loved to spoil each other. Nadia bought Yazmin a Gucci purse with the matching sandals from the Gucci store, while Yazmin purchased Nadia the latest Chanel clutch bag. The two enjoyed a wonderful lobster dinner on Ocean Drive before heading back to their suite. Nadia couldn't wait to have Yazmin bent over the balcony tonight. She loved how Yazmin's plump ass looked in the air while she licked and sucked on her from behind. Nadia couldn't get enough of Yazmin. Unbeknownst to everyone, even her husband, Nadia had been bisexual for years. She knew at a young age she had a desire for women when she used to secretly watch other girls in the shower after gym. Nadia's first orgasm was actually by her college roommate. She had been with several women over the years, but none were like Yazmin. Nadia had secretly wanted Yazmin from the first day she walked in the bank and saw her. Her rudeness toward her, was only to stop her from acting on her feelings. Nadia would watch Yazmin's ass sway from side to side as she walked around her job; and hoped one day she would have a taste. Her wish had finally come true. Nadia was in love with Yazmin and would stop at nothing to make Yazmin hers.

The weekend flew by, and before Yazmin and Nadia knew it, they were enjoying their last day in Miami. As they sat on the balcony and sipped mimosas, each lady was consumed in their own thoughts. Yazmin was nervous and excited about her boutique's grand opening in a few days, and Nadia was dreading her husband's release from prison next week. Although Nadia still had love for Dre, she no longer desired to be with him. The final straw was finding out Dre had fathered a child during their marriage. During Nadia's last visit with Dre he confessed to having a six-year-old child with another woman. The same woman Nadia had been in several altercations with over the years, leading to her being placed on probation for assault charges. Nadia remembered the day she was arrested like it was yesterday. *Nadia and Dre had spent the entire day at the mall Christmas shopping for their family and friends. The smell of cinnamon tickled Nadia's nose as they walked past Cinnaworld. Nadia felt her stomach growl and realized she hadn't eaten anything since breakfast and decided to treat herself to a cinnamon roll. With Dre's arm wrapped around her waist, they made their way over to the counter to place their order. Just as they were about to order a woman approached them. "Who the fuck is this bitch Dre?" the woman asked, before shoving Dre. Nadia didn't know who the woman was and didn't care. She had placed her hands on her man, and where Nadia came from, that was a definite no-no. Before Dre could react, Nadia grabbed the woman by her ponytail, slung her to the ground and repeatedly kicked and stomped her in the face. The next thing Nadia knew she was in handcuffs and sitting in the back of a police cruiser, while the EMS tended to the woman's injuries. Nadia would later learn through court procedures the woman's name was Kam and that she had been in a relationship with Dre for years, eventually having his son. Over the next few years, Kam and Nadia would have several encounters, which included Kam slashing the tires of Nadia's car and Nadia busting out Kam's house windows, all while Dre vowed Kam was nothing more than a delusional, psychopath that was infatuated with him. Nadia knew in her heart Dre was lying but she could never prove it. She went through Dre's phone on a regular basis and never found one call or text message as evidence. Dre had been careful, but not careful enough, by getting Kam pregnant.*

Chapter 6

As Nadia finished the last of her mimosa, she sat her glass down and turned to Yazmin. It was now or never; Nadia was finally ready to make Yazmin hers. Grabbing Yazmin by the hand, Nadia looked her in the eyes and told her how much she loved her and wanted them to spend the rest of their lives together. Yazmin took another sip of her mimosa and fell into a fit of giggles. When she noticed that she was the only one laughing, she immediately stopped. Yazmin couldn't believe Nadia was serious. Did she really think they could just run off into the sunset without a care in the world? They were both married with children. What would their kids think? Yazmin came from a Christian family, her father was a minister and would be appalled to even know Yazmin was having a sexual relationship with another woman, let alone being in a relationship with one. And she most certainly would not hurt Terry's pride by leaving him for another woman. Although Yazmin knew she was wrong for sleeping with Nadia; in her mind she justified her behavior by Nadia being a woman. Nadia had tried to use a strap-on on several different occasions, but Yazmin always refused. Yazmin only considered the act of "penetration" cheating. She admits, her and Terry's marriage was rocky, but she wasn't ready to throw in the towel as of yet. Yazmin loved Nadia, but she couldn't see herself in a full relationship with her or any other woman for that matter. She knew once she explained all of this to Nadia their friendship would probably end. She didn't want to lose Nadia, but she knew their friendship couldn't continue knowing how Nadia felt about her. As the two women cried and embraced, Nadia assured Yazmin she understood. The two spent the rest of the day, enjoying each other between the sheets, because they both knew this would be their last time.

~ One Year Later ~

Yazmin rolled over and grabbed her phone off the nightstand to stop her alarm from going off. Once again, she woke up in bed, alone. She couldn't remember the last time her and Terry had woken up in the same bed and their sex life had become practically nonexistent. She sighed as she slipped on her house shoes and headed downstairs. She knew just where she would find Terry; passed out in the family room. She tripped over two beer bottles entering the room. Terry was passed out on the couch in his boxers, with a drumstick in his hand. The plate of food Yazmin had left in the microwave for him the night before was splattered across the floor. She let out a frustrated scream looking at the gravy stains that were now embedded in her beautiful white carpet. Terry stirred but did not wake up. His drinking was becoming worse by the day. She had repeatedly tried to get him into some type of alcoholic anonymous program, but he refused to go. Terry denied having a problem, which led to frequent arguments in their home. Between Terry's drinking problem and Yazmin's mother's failing health, she was slowly slipping into a state of depression. Yazmin missed having Nadia as a shoulder to cry on. She had not spoken to her in over a year after they both agreed no communication was best. Yazmin would come across Nadia's pictures on Facebook from time to time and wondered how things were going since her husband came home. As she turned to leave the room and get ready for work, Yazmin took one last look at Terry, with drool and dried up gravy around his mouth and shook her head. She no longer cared to help someone who didn't care to help themselves.

Chapter 7

The room felt like it was spinning in circles as Terry tried to sit up. He looked at the clock on the cable box and tried to focus in on the time. When he was finally able to make out the little red numbers, he jumped up in alarm. Terry dashed out the family room and up the stairs into the master bedroom. The bed was neatly made up with his work clothes laid out in the middle of it. He instantly felt ashamed as he stomped back down the stairs. Another night he had left his wife to sleep alone, while he was passed out drunk. Terry's job as a district manager with one of the top distribution companies in the state, often required him to work long hours. He was blessed to have a wife who made sure he had a homecooked meal left in the microwave every night when he finally made it home from work. Terry was infatuated with Yazmin the moment he saw her. *"You have one ahead of you fam." His barber, Matt said, when he walked into the barber shop. Terry nodded his head as he walked past the pool table in the middle of the floor and headed to the back of the shop to play a game of darts. "Your aim sucks," he heard a small squeaky voice say from behind him. Terry turned, expecting to see a mousy looking female to match the high pitch voice, instead he was facing a sexy, caramel woman with a gorgeous smile. "Hi, I'm Yazmin, Matt's sister," she said, extending her hand. "You have to bend your arm like this," picking up a dart and throwing it. Terry was impressed when the dart landed right on the bullseye. The next few darts Terry threw, all landed on the bullseye, while Yazmin cheered him on from the side. He found it refreshing to be around such a down to Earth woman. Most women wouldn't even give him the time of day. It wasn't that he was unattractive; most women just mistook his shyness as being weird. At the age of thirty-five, Terry had dated a few women here and there, but had yet to be in a serious relationship. He was hopeful that*

Yazmin would be the woman to change that. When Terry's barber called for him, the two exchanged numbers and promised to get together soon.

After just six months of dating, Terry proposed to Yazmin. He was ecstatic to have a woman like her to claim as his own, after being rejected by women most of his life. He knew it was wrong and selfish not to disclose the pieces of his past that would surly affect their marriage, but he didn't want to jeopardize losing her.

Thirteen-year-old Terry stood in his bedroom window as he watched his parents back out of the driveway, headed on a seven-day cruise to Jamaica. People often mistook Terry's parents for his grandparents because of how up in age they were. At the age of fifty, Terry's mother received the surprise of her life when she learned she was four months pregnant. Her two oldest children were grown and had already started families of their own. Although she and her husband were shocked, they believed Terry was a gift from God and meant to serve a purpose in their lives. They decided to continue with their retirement plans and although they would not be able to travel as frequently as they originally planned, with the help of family and friends watching Terry, they managed to take at least one trip per year. No sooner than his parents were out of sight, his babysitter for the week, Stacy came bouncing into the room. As she sat down on the side of his bed, Terry heard the bed creak under her weight. Stacy was a chubby girl with a case of severe acne, which caused her to be teased a lot in school. "Hey Terry, guess what I have," she sang, holding up two tickets. Terry's eyes lit up when he noticed they were two front row tickets to the basketball game next week. Terry looked at her curiously; she normally didn't talk to him the entire time she babysat, outside of, "What do you want for lunch and dinner?" She held the tickets closer to Terry's face causing him to nearly drool at the chance of being able to attend. Terry loved basketball but because his parents were now retired and on a fixed income, he never was afforded the luxury of attending any sporting events. Terry knew he would do just about anything for those tickets. "What do I have to do?" he whined. Stacey patted the bed and motioned for Terry to come sit down next to her. When he was within arm's reach of Stacy, she grabbed him and yanked his basketball shorts down. Terry was so stunned, he just stood there. Stacy licked her lips as she marveled at the size of what was between the young boy's legs. He was packing more than boys twice his age. Stacy dropped to her knees and took Terry into her mouth. He knew he shouldn't like what she was doing, but it felt good. Terry felt himself becoming rock hard and growing in length. When he heard Stacy start to gag and choke, he became alarmed and tried to pull away, but she stopped him. Terry suddenly felt the strong urge to pee; the sensation was so powerful he couldn't form any words. As the tingling feeling moved from his toes up through his body, he started to feel faint. Feeling his body rock and jerk, he grabbed ahold of Stacy's head to steady himself. Terry watched numerous porno movies late at night, while his parents thought he was asleep, to know he had just experienced his first orgasm. When the last of Terry's seeds had left his body, Stacy pulled his still hard piece out of her mouth and smiled. "My turn!" she wickedly said as she stood and took off her clothes. "It's time for you to earn them tickets!" she told him as she laid across the bed and spread her legs as far as they would go. Terry backed away from her huge hairy pussy. "Do you want your parents to know what you just let me do to you?" she angrily asked. Terry quickly shook his head no. He breathed a sigh of relief when Stacy got up and left the room. Just as he bent over to pick his basketball shorts off the floor, Terry felt a painful smack on the ass! "You won't be needing those anytime soon, drink this!" she demanded, handing him a cup filled with a brown liquid. Terry instantly started gagging from the first sip. Stacy stood there watching him, with her arms folded across her chest as he took a few more sips. When she thought he had enough, Stacy took the cup from him, sat it on the floor and hopped back on the bed. This time Terry crawled between her legs and quickly shut his eyes to avoid seeing the clumps of hair between her legs. "Now lick!" she ordered. Terry stuck out his tongue and imitated what he saw men do in the pornos he watched, wiggling his tongue fast and then slow. By the way Stacy was squirming around, he assumed he was doing it right. When she said that's enough, Terry hopped up feeling sick, thrilled to know it was finally over. To his disappointment, Stacy rolled over on her knees. "Put that big dick in!" she commanded. Terry was a virgin and had no idea what he was doing. When Stacy looked back and noticed his confusion, she instructed him to spread her ass cheeks open and look for a hole. Terry did as he was told, and as he pumped in and out of her, he tried not to gag at the sight of Stacy lumpy ass jiggling all over the place. When Stacy screamed, "Right there!" Terry was unsure of what to do, so he started pumping faster. When she screamed and collapsed on the bed, Terry waited on her to tell him what to do next. As Stacy stood and strutted out of the room, she threw the tickets on top of Terry's dresser. "Have fun at the game!" she laughed.

Chapter 8

For the next two years, Stacy lavished Terry with money, gifts, and courtside tickets to every basketball game that came to town, while Terry lavished Stacy with countless orgasms. Terry hated himself for what he was doing, but he didn't stop because he loved the gifts, so he chose to use liquor to rationalize the situation. The older Terry got, the more ashamed he felt of what he was doing. He decided to relocate to a different city for a fresh start. When Terry met Yazmin, he was in love with her beauty, intelligence, and fire. The first time they had sex, Terry came in three minutes. He was beyond embarrassed, but Yazmin thought it was cute and stroked him under the covers to get him back hard. When she got on her knees and wiggled her ass in the air, ready for round two, Terry had an instant flashback of Stacy's lumpy ass in the air and he felt himself instantly deflating. Terry knew Yazmin craved to have her lower lips licked by the way she nudged his head between her legs, when he placed kisses down her body. He wanted to orally please his wife, but the thoughts of Stacy's hairy, sour pussy always invaded his mind, stopping him. Terry was fully aware that he wasn't sexually pleasing his wife, so it came as no surprise to him when he discovered that her and Nadia were more than friends. He had come home early from work one day and overheard his wife having phone sex in their bedroom. Right when Terry was about to barge in the room, Yazmin placed her phone on speaker to get more comfortable and he was shocked to hear Nadia's voice on the other end of the phone. Terry had no idea his wife was attracted to women. At first, he was upset, but after thinking about it, he concluded that if he has been open and honest with his wife in the beginning they would not be in this situation. As much as Yazmin begged him to open up and talk to her he couldn't find the strength to tell her how he used alcohol to cope with his past, and why certain sexual acts repulsed him. If letting another woman lick his wife from time to time was the price he had to pay to keep his dirty secret safe, he was okay with that. Not fully understanding, one secret, led to a thousand more.

Chapter 9

As Yazmin sat at her desk, she began to feel lightheaded and dizzy. Her manager Megan noticed something was wrong and helped Yazmin to the breakroom. Yazmin had been experiencing migraines for the past week and assumed it was due to all the stress she was under. Her boutique was doing so well she had to hire a part time assistant to run the store while she was at work. Megan insisted Yazmin take the rest of the day off; she didn't need Yazmin collapsing at her desk in front of a lobby full of people. Megan liked Yazmin because she was a hard worker and rarely took days off work. Although Yazmin never talked about it, Megan knew Yazmin's mother's health had recently took a turn for the worse. Megan knew the pain of losing a mother and her heart went out to Yazmin. Megan assured Yazmin they could handle the rest of the customers and sent her home for the day. Yazmin grabbed her purse and punched out. She decided to run in the grocery store next door to her job and grab some juice and soup, before heading home. While she did feel bad for leaving work early, Yazmin looked forward to going home and cuddling under her blankets with her Kindle. She was just getting to the good part of *"In Love with Her Man"* by Linette King. She could hardly put the book down; it was so good. Yazmin was so deep in thought, she wasn't paying attention to where she was going and crashed into something so hard, she flew back and landed right on her ass in the middle of the store. She was so embarrassed she didn't even want to look up, but when she did, her eyes landed on a face so gorgeous it had to be sent straight from God. As the man extended his hand to help her up, Yazmin couldn't help but to marvel at the stranger's muscular physique, filled with tattoos. She quickly turned away from the man's outstretched hand and started quickly gathering up the items that had spilled from her purse during the impact of her fall. Yazmin could feel the man's eyes on her and tried to get away from his uncomfortable stare as fast as possible. She decided to grab the items she needed elsewhere. Walking out the store, she snuck a glance behind her and just as she thought, the mysterious man was still watching her. Damn he's fine, Yazmin thought, as she continued to her car. Something about him seemed a little familiar, but she couldn't put her finger on it. Yazmin fantasized about the stranger all the way home, as she imagined how many positions those strong arms could flip her into. "Stop it girl!" she scolded herself, but still couldn't get the stranger off her mind. For the rest of the day, Yazmin laid in bed, reading and getting caught up on her rest.

Chapter 10

It was a beautiful Saturday in Michigan for early April. Customers were in and out of Yazmin's boutique all day looking for a fly outfit to go out and floss in. One thing you could count on in Detroit; the minute the sun came out, the niggas did too. The malls, parks, and streets were full of people out enjoying the day because there was no telling when the next nice day would be. Yazmin looked around her boutique feeling extremely proud of her biggest accomplishment. After years of saving and planning, her dream of owning her own clothing store had finally come true. She had decorated the store in her favorite colors, gold and silver. The huge crystal chandelier that hung from the ceiling gave the store an elegant touch, while the fuzzy rugs spread throughout the store provided a nice and cozy vibe. Yazmin's favorite piece of furniture in the entire store was the marble custom-made desk with her initials trimmed in silver and gold her father purchased as a congratulation gift for her. She was blessed to have a supportive family. While it deeply hurt Yazmin that Terry had yet made the time to come see her store, she refused to dwell on it, or let it ruin her moment. She turned up the radio and jammed to old school R&B, as she put away inventory. Just as Yazmin was almost done, she looked up and saw an elderly delivery guy pushing a cart full of roses into the store. There were so many roses on the cart, he was having a hard time pushing it. Yazmin tried to stop him before he made his way completely into the store. There must have been some type of mistake. It was no way anybody she knew would send a small fortune of roses to her. Yazmin lowered the volume on the radio, as she politely told the gentleman he had the wrong store. The elderly man looked confused as he stepped back outside the store and looked from the card he held in his hand, to the sign across the front of the store. He stepped back in and smiled, as he gave Yazmin a form to sign. Yazmin glanced down at the form, which indeed had her name, along with her boutique's name on it. She signed the slip of paper, while admiring the roses in all different colors. Her heart swelled as she ripped open the card expecting to see a message from Terry congratulating her on the grand opening of her store. Although he had not physically made it to the store, it still warmed Yazmin's heart to know Terry had done something so beautiful to show he was indeed happy for her. Yazmin frowned in confusion as she read the card, *"Congratulations to a beautiful woman, doing beautiful things! I would love to get to know you better!" Love Jai!* Yazmin said the name over and over in her head but could not come up with anybody she knew by that name. Just as she had given up hope on trying to figure the mystery out, the handsome man she crashed into at the store the other day walked in. As Yazmin stood there stunned, the man, who she now knew was the mysterious Jai, grabbed her around the waist and pulled her close to him. As if reading her mind, Jai leaned in and whispered in her ear, "I always have a way to find and get what I want!" Jai aggression would have scared any other woman but not Yazmin, instead it turned her on. Yazmin's mind screamed run, but it's hard to follow your mind, when your body's desires are taking you into a totally different direction. Jai convinced Yazmin to close the boutique early and join him for dinner. They decided on Starters, a small neighborhood bar that had excellent food with a cozy, chill atmosphere, where the two could talk, and get to know each other better.

Chapter 11

Over dinner, Yazmin learned Jai's government name was Jai'andre Daniels and he was a thirty-five-year-old business investor. He explained to her, the day they collided into each other at the store, she had left one of her boutique flyers on the ground, while hurrying to gather the spilled belongings from her purse. When Jai noticed the flyer on the ground, he couldn't help but to pick it up and stuff it in his back pants pocket. There was something about Yazmin that made Jai curious. He never chased any woman; they threw themselves at him all day, every day. Jai was buried knee deep in different pussy every night, he was that nigga and he knew it. Whoever said light skin men were played out, hadn't come across him. His 6'1", tattooed muscular frame commanded attention whenever he walked into a room. Jai never left the house without having on at least a thousand-dollar outfit and the most expensive cologne money could buy. Whatever woman he wanted, he got, and right now Yazmin was who he had his eyes set on. Jai knew right away Yazmin would be a challenge for him. He could tell she wasn't the typical weak bitch he was used too, including his wife. Jai and his wife were separated, but had to stay married, at least on paper, until Jai got off of parole. Jai had paroled to his wife's address because his supervising agent would be conducting monthly home visits as a required condition of his parole. It barely took five minutes into their first visit, for Jai to realize his parole agent, Mack was one of those square, bullied as a child, uptight assholes who would make his time on parole a living hell. As Agent Mack rattled off a long list of violations that he wouldn't hesitate to have Jai locked back up for, Jai grunted in torment. When Jai noticed the geeky parole agent's eyes lock in on his wife's ass hanging from the bottom of her denim booty shorts every time she walked by, he came up with a plan. As Agent Mack sat on the couch and filled out a few forms, Jai slyly sent his wife a text message. A few minutes later, Jai's wife walked into the living room naked and stood in front of the agent, rubbing her hard nipples as Jai leaned back in his chair to get a better view. Jai smirked to himself when he noticed the look on the Agent Mack's face. He had the typical *"I'm about to fuck up,"* grimace a man makes when he is fighting the battle of thinking with his big head or little head, but his little head is winning. As Jai's wife dropped to her knees and unbuckled Agent Mack's pants, Jai knew he had him right where he wanted, when he did nothing to stop her. Jai's wife took Agent Mack into her warm mouth and begin gently sucking him, causing him to drop the forms he was filling out and squeal out in pure delight. As her head bobbed up and down on his lap, Jai and his agent sat across from each other and "revised" his parole conditions. The agent agreed he would overlook all of Jai parole restrictions, including drug testing, enforcing his curfew and the mandatory job requirement; in return the agent would fuck Jai's wife every month, during his routine home visit. As Agent Mack filled Jai's wife mouth with his cum, he happily agreed to their new arrangement. He was enjoying the moment so much, he never noticed Jai snapping a few pictures for a little reassurance, just in case he tried to back out of their deal later. For the past year, the arrangement had been working out perfect. Jai enjoyed his freedom while being on parole and Agent Mack enjoyed Jai's wife goods once a month, while he watched and even joined in on a few occasions. Jai didn't feel bad one bit that he was pimping his wife out to his parole agent, he was amused that it didn't matter how bad he treated her, she would still do anything he wanted. Jai always felt once you gain control over a woman's mind, you can control everything else about her. If a weak bitch was going to let him use her, he would use them every chance he got, including his wife, and his new love interest Yazmin.

Yazmin sat at her desk scrolling through Facebook. The gloomy and rainy day had kept everyone inside, making it an easy money day at the job. "Excuse me ma'am?" a very deep voice said from across the counter. Yazmin hesitated a moment before looking up. "Can't people read!" she muttered under her breath. The sign in the middle of the lobby clearly said please wait to be called next. When Yazmin finally looked up, she came face to face with a huge bouquet of roses. Jai slowly lowered the flowers down and flashed his beautiful smile. "For you," he said. Yazmin blushed and looked around, as her nosey co-workers openly gawked at her. It was against company rules to accept gifts from customers. "I can't accept those," she whispered. "I'll get in trouble!" Jai went and sat the vase of flowers on the table in the back of the lobby. "What are you doing here?" she giggled. "I'm a customer," he said in a fake professional tone. Jai sat his briefcase on the counter and pulled out two checks. "I need to deposit these into my account and make a withdrawal." Yazmin took the checks from Jai and began to enter the information into her computer as they flirted over the counter. The two made plans to have dinner later that evening. "Girl who is that?" her co-worker Natalie rushed up to her and asked as Jai excited the building. "Trouble," she smiled. As both women admired Jai walking away through the huge glass window, Natalie leaned in and whispered, "I'll take that punishment any day!" For the rest of the day Yazmin couldn't keep Jai off her mind. He was everything she desired in a man; sexy, romantic, confident, with just the right amount of swag. Too bad everything that glitters isn't gold.

Chapter 12

"This shit fire!" Shotta said, as he took another puff of the weed before handing it to Jai. The smoke was so thick in the living room, the two men could barely see each other. Shotta was one of the few people Jai trusted. They grew up in the same neighborhood and even though they had a ten-year age difference, they were thick as thieves. Jai laughed, thinking about the day they met. He had been playing basketball in front of his house when a money green, old school Chevrolet on gold rims, came burling around the corner and stopped right in front of his house. A thin, skinny man with dreads jumped out of the car and dashed over to the bushes on the side of Jai's house. Jai silently watched as the man bent down and jammed something into the dirt. He was unsure what to do when the man jogged over to him and told him to bounce him the ball, while wiping sweat off his forehead. Jai hesitated for a moment, but when he noticed the police cruiser turning the same corner the Chevy had just came from, Jai bounced him the ball. Before either one of them could say one word, the two police officers known as "Frick and Frat," throughout the neighborhood, jumped out of the police car, grabbed the dread head man and roughly threw him on the hood of their squad car. "What you got for us?" Frick chuckled. Jai silently looked on in curiosity, as the two officers intrusively searched the man. After coming up empty handed, they ran his name hoping to find a reason to take him in. They were thrilled when they discovered the man had a warrant for unpaid tickets. As they handcuffed him and threw him in the back of the police cruiser, the man slightly nodded his head at Jai when they made eye contact, right before the police cruiser pulled off. As soon as they were out of sight, Jai immediately ran and began searching the car. He stuffed the wad of money and cell phone he found in his pocket, before rolling up the windows and locking the car doors. Next, he went over to the bushes and dug his fingers around in the dirt. When he felt the plastic bag brush across his fingertips, he gently pulled the bag out. He took everything inside the house and hid it in an old shoe box in the back of his closet. Jai was young, but he was wise for his age. He laid across his bed and smiled. Jai knew if he played this situation right, it would be his chance to jump head first in the game. Jai had secretly watched the dread head man for months, as he slowly took over several trap houses in the neighborhood and he wanted in. His mother was a single parent that did her best to provide for him, but Jai wanted more. The flashy cars and designer clothes had always intrigued him and now was his chance to get in on the action. Jai took notice of how all the women in the neighborhood flocked to the dope boys on the block with money. Day after day, he witnessed women embarrass, degrade, and humiliate themselves for a quick dollar. Growing up, Jai saw firsthand how women are controlled by money, and their craving for attention. He would never forget the day he learned this the hard way. *Every day after school, Jai would walk his crush, Jasmine, home while carrying her books and telling her corny jokes. Jai had been saving all his money from his summer job to buy Jasmine a nice birthday present. He admired the silver bracelet he had purchased with his hard-earned money, as he walked to her house. As Jai stepped up on the porch, something in the living room window caught his eye. Jasmine was on her knees giving head to one of the block corner boys. When she looked up and saw Jai looking through the window, she ran to the door trying to explain. "I'm sorry Jai, but you can't afford me," she boldly said. Jai didn't say a word, as he threw the bracelet he brought on the ground and stormed off the porch.* From that day on, he vowed to treat bitches how they deserved to be treated. Jai was prepared when the dread head knocked on his front door a few days later after being released from jail. Jai didn't say a word as he opened the door and headed to his room. Once he retrieved the shoe box from the back of the closet, he went back into the living room and handed the dread head the box. Jai stood quietly off to the side as the man examined each item in the box. He smiled as he noticed the young boy had not only removed all his valuable items from the car and safely put them away, he had also retrieved the drugs he had stashed as well. Shotta was even more impressed when he counted the money left in the car and every dime was there. He threw the wad of money to Jai. "That's for being a real nigga! Welcome to the family," he coolly said. The two had been hustling and getting money together ever since. Jai thought about the new caramel beauty he had just met. Yazmin was wifey material, she was smart, pretty, fun, motivated and had goals. If he wasn't careful, she would distract him from their plans. "Money over bitches," was their number one rule!

Chapter 13

"Is everything going according to plan?" Shotta asked taking the blunt back from Jai. The weed haze had both men feeling good and ready to talk business. Jai reached into his pocket and pulled out half of the money from the checks he had cashed earlier at Yazmin's job. "Off and running," he grinned. The two men were always on the lookout for new scams and hustles to make money. Marijuana was becoming legal in almost every state, causing dispensaries to pop up on nearly every street corner. With people now having the option to purchase their drugs in clean and safe environments, as opposed to on street corners in risky neighborhoods, for only a few extra dollars, corner boys and trap houses were quickly becoming a thing of the past so Jai and Shotta moved on to the next best thing, counterfeit checks. After studying a few YouTube videos and purchasing thousands of dollars worth of equipment, the two had quickly developed an elaborate counterfeit check business. The checks were printed on the highest quality paper money could buy, making it almost impossible to detect they were phony. Every now and then they would come across a prissy white bitch, who would flag one of their checks and put a hold on the account they used. Whenever this happened, they would just move on to the next bank. After having a check flagged one too many times, they came up with a plan. Jai had always been able to charm a woman into doing whatever he wanted. They just needed to find the perfect teller for him to work on his magic on. Jai and Yazmin bumping into each other in the store that day wasn't by accident, Jai had actually arranged the whole incident to spark up a conversation with her. In fact, Yazmin hadn't dropped her boutique flyer at all that day. Jai knew exactly where her boutique was because he had been watching her for months. Jai would sit in the back of Yazmin's job for hours and watch her. He could tell

Yazmin was lonely and desperate for attention and knew sending the flowers would reel her right in. Yazmin was going to make Jai a lot of money once he broke her down and trained her like he had done all his other bitches.

Over the next few months Jai devoted all his free time to Yazmin. Jai knew Yazmin wasn't the type of women you could impress with gifts, so he showered her with attention instead. Jai would bring lunch to Yazmin's job every day, plan picnics on the weekend and help her out around the boutique. All Yazmin's customers loved Jai; he would often imitate Jody off "Baby Boy," oohing in admiration every time a woman stepped out the dressing room. One spin around by Jai followed by telling her how good she looked in the outfit was all it took for them to be completely sold on the outfit. Jai increased the boutique's sells so much at the store that Yazmin considered putting him on her payroll. She had become completely smitten with Jai. He became the shoulder she needed to lean on. Although the two had yet to have sex, their chemistry was amazing. Terry and Yazmin had pretty much become just roommates. Terry had moved into the guest room and the two only spoke in passing. As Yazmin and Terry grew more distant, Yazmin and Jai became closer. In her mind, Yazmin had finally met the man of her dreams; what Yazmin didn't know was Jai was becoming impatient by the day. The more time passed, the harder it was for Jai to keep up his "good guy" act. Jai had spent thousands of dollars on roses, expensive lunch and dinner dates and the countless spa trips Yazmin loved and had yet to still sample her goods. Jai got hard just thinking of how tight Yazmin's walls were when he stuck his finger in her the other day, while making out in the jacuzzi at the spa. Just when he was about to slip inside her, Yazmin stopped him and jacked him off instead. That pleased Jai for the moment, but it wouldn't for long. Jai didn't expect for the first part of his plan to take so long. He was anxious to move on with the plan, and even more anxious to dive knee deep between Yazmin's legs.

Chapter 14

Yazmin and Jai were enjoying an afternoon cuddling and watching movies in their downtown hotel room. Jai sat at the edge of the bed with Yazmin's feet in his lap alternating between rubbing her feet and legs. Yazmin's soft moans let him know she was enjoying the massage. Jai scooted toward the middle of the bed and begin to rub further up Yazmin's leg. As he pushed the thin sundress she was wearing up, he could feel the heat coming from between Yazmin's legs. He marveled at the sight of juicy peach through the white lace panties she wore. Jai looked up at Yazmin and admired how beautiful and peaceful she looked with her head laid back on the pillow and a soft smile on her face. He reached up and slowly slid her panties down over her thick hips. He slid his finger over Yazmin's wetness, as she spread her legs a little to give him more access. On cue, Jai slid between Yazmin's legs and replaced his finger with his tongue. Yazmin's eyes popped open in surprise but it was too late, there was no escaping the powerful grip Jai had on her hips. As Jai licked slow circles around her opening, she sighed in pure bliss. Jai alternated between licks and swirls on her clit, causing Yazmin's body to erupt in trembles from an orgasm within minutes. She tried to wiggle out of Jai's grip, but he was too strong for her. Jai kept licking until Yazmin's body was shaking from her second orgasm. As he slid from between her legs, he grew harder seeing her juices soaking the sheets. Suddenly, Yazmin sat up and attempted to pull her dress down. Jai couldn't believe Yazmin was trying to be on this "I'm not ready," shit again. In a flash, Jai pushed Yazmin back on the bed and ripped off the thin sundress with one swift pull. Before Yazmin could utter one word he leaned in and forcefully started kissing her, pushing his tongue down her throat as far as it would go. When Yazmin begin to return the kiss, Jai eased her back and slid inside her, before she could object. Jai had to muffle a moan as he placed Yazmin's leg on his shoulder and grinded into her. Jai now believed Yazmin was being honest when she told him she hadn't slept with her husband in months because of how incredibly tight she was. Jai knew he was hitting Yazmin's spot when her leg began to tremble on his shoulder. He reached down and begin to rub her clit in a soft circular motion, while she came, never losing the rhythm of his stroke. Yazmin begin to mumble incoherently as a stream of fluid came flying out of her. Yazmin had heard of women squirting before but until now she didn't know her body could. Jai felt his nut rising and just when he was about to cum, he pulled out and flipped Yazmin on her stomach. Placing Yazmin's ass in the air as far as it would go Jai eased himself back into her. Jai marveled at the sight of Yazmin's plump caramel ass in the air, jiggling with every stroke he made. He felt his breathing speed up as Yazmin used her walls to grip him. Jai gave her ass two hard smacks right before he pulled out and came on her back. Jai collapsed on the bed as Yazmin snuggled up against him. Jai was in a daze; he wasn't expecting sex with Yazmin to be so good. He was now starting to second guess his original plan.

Chapter 15

The day of Yazmin's mother's funeral went by in a blur. Yazmin's mother's health condition had improved so much over the last few months her doctor had just given her the okay to be released from the hospital and finish all her treatments outpatient, at home. The night before her mother was scheduled to be released from the hospital, she developed a high fever and was diagnosed with a bacterial infection; less than twenty-four hours later, she was dead. Yazmin's mother's unexpected death was a huge blow to the family, especially for Yazmin's dad. It broke her heart to see her father so hurt. She stayed strong throughout the day while making her mother's funeral arrangements and tending to her father's needs but fell apart the minute she got home. Surprisingly, Terry had took some time off work and cut down on his drinking to console his wife while she grieved. After spending the day finalizing her mother's funeral arrangements, Yazmin was mentally exhausted and ready to crawl into bed. As soon as she opened the front door to her home, the aroma of steak instantly made her stomach rumble, reminding her she had not stopped and ate all day. As Yazmin followed the delicious smell, she came to a sudden halt when she entered the dining room. On the table was a beautiful candlelight dinner set for two. Yazmin admired the huge crystal vase filled with flowers as tears filled her eyes. Instant guilt washed over her as Terry approached her from behind and wrapped his arm around her waist. Terry could feel he was losing his wife and prayed it wasn't too late to save his marriage. The two enjoyed a quiet dinner, while jazz played softly in the background. Yazmin welcomed the peaceful silence after such a long day and felt a calming sense of peace. As she looked across the table at her husband, Yazmin did something she hadn't done in a while, she silently prayed. Yazmin prayed for forgiveness of her sins, and the strength to fight off her fleshly desires. As she laid on Terry's chest later that night, listening to his heartbeat she decided to end things with Jai and work on her marriage. Unfortunately, Jai wouldn't be willing to let her go just that easy.

Chapter 16

"Oh my God Jai, Wait!" Harmony screamed as she tried to pry herself from his grip. Jai ignored her pleas as he forcefully held her by the back of her neck with one hand while spreading her ass cheeks further apart with the other one. Harmony smothered her face in the pillow and tried her best not to tense up as Jai penetrated her anally. Harmony was a thick, half black/half Japanese, big booty stripper that Jai added to his collection of women a year ago, when he first came home from prison. Between her honey colored skin, Chinese slanted eyes, and crazy mouth skills, Harmony had become one of Jai's favorite past times, when he wasn't busy chasing that stupid bitch Yazmin. Jai instantly got mad and started to grind harder in and out of Harmony, as he thought of Yazmin and their last conversation. *Jai knew something was up when Yazmin asked him to meet her at their favorite bar to talk. While sipping on her long island, Yazmin told Jai she had decided to try to fix her marriage and could no longer see him. As Jai picked up his beer and took a swig to calm himself, he was fuming on the inside, "Who did this bitch think she was?" he wondered. Although he had originally sought Yazmin for his own selfish reasons, over the last few months he had grown to love her in his own sick way. He had decided to abandon his plan of using her for Shotta and his check scheme and had even went as far as purchasing Yazmin a 4 karat, princess cut, canary yellow diamond engagement ring. After going through her purse one night and finding divorce papers addressed to her husband, Jai was sure their marriage was over. Now the confused bitch wanted to be back with her husband. There was no way in hell Jai was going to let that happen. He had given up too much to be with her. Jai told Yazmin he completely understood as he stood to leave.* Harmony's high pitch squeals snapped Jai back into reality. Jai knew

Harmony was in pain because he didn't bother to use any oil before he forcefully pushed himself further into her tight asshole. Harmony's ass felt like it was going to split in two as she fought back tears. She wouldn't dare tell Jai to stop, for fear of what he would do. As he wrapped his fist around Harmony's thirty-inch Brazilian weave, he pulled and snatched her head viciously taking out all his frustrations on her. "Stop crying bitch and throw that ass back!" Jai commanded, as he slapped Harmony hard across the ass. Harmony's cries of pain combined with the sight of her ass jiggling in the air, had Jai ready to explode. As he pulled out and forced Harmony on her knees, he moaned in pleasure. Once every drop was released, Jai had Harmony clean him up while he lit his blunt and thought of how he was going to get Yazmin back in his life once and for all.

Chapter 17

Yazmin and Terry's happiness was short lived. Terry was back drinking heavy, which put a strain on their marriage once again. As Yazmin walked through the boutique putting away inventory, she fought back tears as she recalled her recent failed attempt to rekindle the flame in her marriage. *Yazmin decided to plan her and Terry an overnight, romantic getaway. She booked the honeymoon suite in a luxurious downtown hotel with a heart shaped jacuzzi and a beautiful view overlooking the Riverfront. She had spent the entire day getting everything ready, so the night would be perfect. Yazmin looked around the suite and smiled as she admired the white and pink rose petals that covered the entire floor throughout the suite. Vanilla scented candles flickered softly around the jacuzzi, leaving just the right romantic touch. Sitting on the table in the middle of the suit was Terry's favorite meal of stuffed lobster, sautéed shrimp, garlic mashed potatoes and buttered rolls. Yazmin had left Terry a personalized invitation that included the address to the hotel, room number and a sexy picture of her with the simple message, "You are invited to come enjoy the night of your life." She placed the envelope in the middle of the bed where he couldn't miss it. As the night grew later and Terry had still yet to arrive, Yazmin began to worry. The food was now ice cold and the candles had completely burned out. After calling his phone for over an hour Yazmin decided to drive home and check on her husband. When she pulled into the driveway, Yazmin noticed Terry's car parked in his normal spot. At first, she thought Terry may have overlooked the envelope on the bed. Yazmin's worry turned into anger, the minute she stepped into their room. Terry laid sprawled across the bed with the open invitation in one hand, and an empty bottle of whiskey in the other. Yazmin reached over and slapped Terry across the face as hard as she could.*

Terry's eyes popped open as he looked around stunned. He had only planned to have one quick drink to loosen up a little and enjoy his night with his wife after opening the invitation she had left on the bed. One drink turned into the whole bottle and he ended up passed out across the bed. As Yazmin stormed from the room crying hysterically, Terry for the first time ever, admitted he needed help. "Ding, Dong" the chime of someone entering the store distracted Yazmin from her thoughts. Yazmin looked up and smiled as Jai stood in the doorway, looking handsome as ever in a black linen suit, complimented by crisp Louis Vuitton loafers. As the two passionately kissed in the middle of the store, all thoughts of Yazmin fixing her marriage went completely out the window.

Yazmin and Jai became inseparable. Yazmin filed for divorce but still lived in the home she and Terry shared. Jai hated this and slowly began to show his insecure side by often accusing Yazmin of still sleeping with her husband. Yazmin thought Jai's jealous behavior was cute when everyone else saw it as a warning sign. Jai was obsessed with Yazmin; and the thought of another man touching her, husband or not, sent him into a state of rage. Yazmin had no idea that Jai had followed her home from work one day to find out where she lived. He had parked down the street from her house on several different occasions and watched Terry leave out for work. Jai was from the streets and knew he could easily have Terry eliminated out the picture, but because Yazmin had recently filed for divorce that would bring a lot of heat to the both, heat Jai didn't need. Jai was tired of playing nice, it was time he made it clear who's bitch Yazmin officially was. For the first time in his life, Jai had met a woman who challenged him and didn't come easy. Yazmin was a good girl and the fact that she wouldn't just do anything he said, like all the other women in his life actually turned him on even more. With Yazmin's encouragement, he had recently opened a detail shop and a car wash. He had always wanted to open a legit business but never had the right insight on how, until now. With Yazmin showing him the ropes, he now had two legitimate businesses up and going. Jai spent the entire next day apartment searching. He knew Yazmin loved her house and he would have to find the perfect apartment to convince her to leave it. Jai found a cozy little two-bedroom apartment five minutes from her job. The apartment included a marble fireplace and a huge balcony right over a pond where she could sit and relax, reading her Kindle books. That was one thing he adored about Yazmin, she still had her innocence. She preferred to be cuddled in her bed reading endless books on her Kindle, than in bars and clubs like all the other hoes he knew. Jai furnished the apartment with an all-white Italian leather living room set, white and gold marble dining room set, and a pearl white California king canopy bed that took up most of the room. Jai hired an interior decorator to come in and put crystal mirrors and vases throughout the apartment. The finishing touch was the huge portrait of Yazmin's mother Jai placed over the fireplace. Jai was positive Yazmin would fall in love with the apartment as soon as she saw it and move in right away.

Chapter 18

"Ride that shit," Jai said, as Yazmin bounced up and down on top of him in the California king size bed. Yazmin had fell in love with the apartment the moment she saw it. With Jai's urging, she moved her stuff in the same day and he had been snuggled between her legs every night since. Jai slightly lifted his body up just enough to slip one of Yazmin's plump nipples into his mouth, but not interrupt her rhythm. The way Yazmin swirled and rocked her hips as she grinded on him was sending him into a frenzy. He was amazed at how she could go from a being a good girl during the day, to a super freak at night. Yazmin had her feet planted firmly on the bed, with her palms flat against the wall over the headboard. She teased him by contracting her muscles around his thickness before spinning around and riding him cowgirl. Jai was in a state of bliss as he held her by her waist and watched her voluptuous ass bouncing up and down. He slyly took one finger and sucked it, before slipping it into her asshole. Yazmin body immediately tensed up from the sudden strange feeling. "Just relax baby!" Jai coaxed, as he slowly moved his finger in and out her hole and stroked her from underneath. Yazmin began to enjoy the double sensation at one time and before she knew it, she was cumming again. Yazmin's body shuddered as a powerful orgasm took over her body. Jai looked down in awe as Yazmin's juices seeped out of her body and oozed down his thighs. He began stroking Yazmin from underneath, damn near sending her into convulsions. She had barely recovered from her last orgasm and was on the verge of having another one. Yazmin tried to maintain control on top but gave up all hope when Jai grabbed her ass and started delivering powerful strokes from below. Jai wanted to slide into her other hole, but he knew she wasn't ready. He would give her a little more time before he demanded she get with the program like all his other bitches.

Jai use to be disgusted by anal sex, that is until his young, little freak bitch from the neighborhood convinced him to try anal sex one day when she was on her period and needed weed. After that, he was turned out. Most of these freaks' walls were stretched out wide as the sea, but their ass was always nice and tight. With their ass hoisted in the air, Jai wouldn't even ask permission before he rammed inside their virgin asshole. Jai got off on their painful screams and desperate attempts to get away from him. As long as a wad of money was left on the dresser, they forgave him and allowed him to violate them over and over again. Jai let out a loud grunt as he held Yazmin's hips releasing his seeds deep into her. As Yazmin collapsed on top of Jai, he thought about Harmony. Jai stroked Yazmin's hair as she drifted off into a deep sleep. He slipped out of bed and quietly got dressed, anxious to go pay Harmony a visit. He needed some good head. They hadn't got that far, but Jai hoped Yazmin could suck a good dick, if not, he had just the right person in mind who would teach her.

Chapter 19

Jai stood in the door of Harmony's bedroom and watched her peacefully sleep. He had demanded she give him a spare key to her house on his first visit. Jai was a narcissist, who required complete control at all times. This was one of the main reasons Jai had rushed to move Yazmin from the house she shared with her husband into an apartment he had access to. Jai needed his woman at his full disposable, twenty-four seven. Women often mistook the things Jai did for them as love, when it was really only for control. Jai sat on the side of the bed and slowly slid the silk sheets down Harmony's flawless body. As he caressed her back, Jai admired her Coca-Cola shape. Harmony was every man's fantasy with her tiny waist, thick thighs, and heart shaped ass. The tiger tattoo that stretched across her entire back made her even sexier. Harmony had potential; she was beautiful, smart, funny and even had a degree in nursing. She worked as a nurse during the day and danced at night to cover her mother's excessive medical bills. Harmony's mother was a Japanese, illegal immigrant, who was disowned by her family when she was announced she was four months pregnant with Harmony, by a black man. From that point on they refused to acknowledge her and acted like she never existed. Harmony's mother and father moved into a small apartment and settled into a comfortable life. Her father hustled and worked cash paying jobs under the table to provide for their family, while her mother stayed at home and took care of the house and kids. When Harmony's father was killed three years ago during a drug transaction, she took over the role of provider for her family. Her mother was diagnosed with cancer a short time later and Harmony started dancing to cover her medical expenses. Harmony felt Jai didn't respect her because she was a stripper. She bent over backwards to prove to him it was more to her than that. She knew the way Jai degraded her was wrong, but she loved him and hoped they would one day be together. Just like all the other women in Jai's life, she thought if she tried hard enough, she could change him. To Jai, Harmony was nothing more than a trophy who boasted his ego. Jai took pride in knowing every man in the club wanted her, but she was his bitch. Harmony only gave lap dances to Jai. He loved the jealous stares men gave him while watching her grind back and forth on him, wishing it was them. To Jai, females were all just temporary bitches, to be used for his benefit, and disposed of when he had no more use for them. Harmony awoke from her sleep to the feel of a hard smack on her ass. She rolled over and stared at the man who had once captured her heart. When they first met Harmony thought she had found her knight in shining armor.

Harmony had met Jai one night while dancing at the strip club where she worked. The mysterious man who flooded the stage with money while she flipped upside down on the pole had instantly grabbed her attention. Harmony finished her set and sexily crawled across the stage to gather the huge amount of money scattered everywhere, mostly thrown by the strange man sitting in front of the stage. As she passed him heading to the dressing room, he grabbed her arm and told her to meet him out front in ten minutes. Harmony was shocked at how bold the man was for automatically assuming she would easily leave with him. Harmony slightly pulled away, being sure not to alert security, "I make three thousand dollars a night, unless you can give me that right now, I'm not going anywhere," she smirked. Harmony was the upscale club's number one money maker; her half Japanese features gave her an exotic look the black men loved, while her huge ass kept the white men in awe. Harmony always went the extra mile in whatever she did, so she took yoga classes for more flexibility on the pole and hip-hop classes to learn the art of "twerking." Two minutes of Harmony's huge ass upside down on the pole twerking in a full split and the club was in an uproar, with the stage full of money. Harmony didn't perform lap dances or private V.I.P. room requests, she didn't have to, all her money was easily made on stage. As Harmony turned to walk away the man slipped something in her hand, Harmony looked down and saw a large wad on money. Full of confidence, he didn't wait on Harmony to respond as he turned and walked away. Twenty minutes later, Harmony was sitting comfortably in the front seat of the man's BMW. Jai took the back of her hand and softly kissed it; the rest was history.

Chapter 20

As Jai stood up and started to undress, Harmony glanced over at the clock and noticed it was three o'clock in the morning. She wondered how Jai had managed to slip away from his precious girlfriend Yazmin so late at night but didn't dare to ask; she knew all too well the consequences that came along with asking too many questions. While Jai finished undressing, Harmony dashed to the kitchen, grabbed two shots of patron and the blunt she had rolled for him earlier. She always kept a freshly rolled blunt ready for Jai's nightly visits. By the time she got back to the room, Jai was naked and propped up against the headboard stroking himself. Harmony sat the shots down on the nightstand, lit the blunt and handed it to him. Once she knew he was comfortable, she crawled between his legs and begin to stroke him. Once he was nice and hard, she stuck her tongue out and swirled it around the tip, before taking him completely into her mouth. The smell of fresh sex coming from Jai's pubic hairs instantly filled her nostrils. He didn't even have enough fuckin respect for her to wash his dirty dick off before coming to put it in her mouth. For months, Harmony foolishly believed she was Jai's one and only. She did everything she could to please him, including the painful anal sex that left her ass on fire for days. Harmony would never forget the first time Jai's second personality reared its ugly head. *Harmony was on her knees slurping and sucking on Jai like a popsicle when his phone began to ring. Jai picked up the phone while still stroking the back of her hair. Harmony suddenly stopped when she heard Jai say, "Hey baby, I'm in a meeting, I'll hit you right back!" and quickly hung up the phone. Harmony stood to her feet so fast she almost lost her balance. She swung on Jai, just missing punching him in the face by inches! "You talking to a bitch while I'm sucking your dick?" she screamed in his face. Jai grabbed*

Harmony and slammed her to the floor. He placed his hand around her neck and applied pressure. "Don't you ever call my woman a bitch again," he spat, while Harmony gasped for air. Jai stopped applying pressure when Harmony's eyes began to roll to the back of her head. "Her name is Yazmin, and if you ever disrespect her in any way, I'll kill you!" Jai calmly stated. By the look in his eyes, Harmony knew Jai meant every word he said. Jai sat back down and instructed her to come finish what she started. "Fuck you Jai, get out!" she screamed. Harmony didn't know what to expect when Jai begin to laugh and reached for his phone. He punched in a few things and Harmony's heart dropped when he tuned the phone in her direction.

Her mother's beautiful picture with the bold word "Wanted" filled Jai's iPhone screen. He had done a little research on little Ms. Harmony. He always checked out the background of any bitch whose house he laid his head at. Jai had done a lot of dirt in his past and couldn't take the chance of getting comfortable with a chic, who turned out to be an acquaintance of someone he had done dirty before.

Imagine his surprise when he discovered Harmony's mother was wanted back in Japan for a hit and run accident that killed an elderly man years ago. Her parents had fled the country before she could be arrested. "Now, unless you want me to get immigration on the phone, bitch get on your knees and finish what you started," Jai angrily spat. The thought of her mother being deported with stage four cancer made Harmony sick to the stomach. She looked into Jai's eyes and saw nothing but evil. Harmony crawled over to Jai and took him back into her mouth. She tried her best not to gag as Jai held on to the sides of her face and pumped hard in and out of her mouth. Just when Harmony felt her jaws about to lock up, Jai hissed, "I'm about to come." Harmony tried to pull her head back, but Jai still had a firm grip on her face. "You about to catch all this shit." Jai evilly grinned. Harmony had never swallowed *before and the sudden fluid hitting the back of her throat caught her off guard. Tears flowed down her face as she tried not to choke on his seeds.* Harmony endured Jai's bipolar behavior hoping he would one day change. One day he was threatening to report her mother to immigration and the next day he was sending her mother flowers and paying for her medical treatment. Jai was an expert at building women up, giving them just enough hope to keep them hanging on, then tearing them back down to maintain control.

Chapter 21

Jai sulked in his seat while Yazmin drove around the huge complex looking for her son's apartment building. Although she had been there a couple of times before she still managed to get lost every time she visited. Yazmin knew Jai had an attitude, but she was not in the mood to deal with it today. If she didn't know better, she would think Jai was jealous of her kids. Every time she brought them something, he would complain about her spoiling grown men. Yazmin's kids were her pride and joy. If they were doing what they were supposed to, she would help them out along the way. Yazmin worked hard for her money and would spend it any way she wanted to, regardless of what anybody had to say. She let out a frustrated sigh before turning to Jai and asking him to open the glove box and hand her the slip of paper that had her son's address on it, "We will probably find it faster if we put it in the GPS," she snapped. When Jai didn't move to retrieve the paper, she angrily reached over him grabbed it herself. "How long are we going to be here?" Jai mumbled. Yazmin ignored him as she typed in the address on her GPS and threw the paper back in the glove box. He could sit his ass in the car for all she cared, she didn't ask him to come in the first place. At first Yazmin relished in how much time Jai wanted to spend with her. Now the constant pop ups at her job and boutique and wanting to go everywhere she went was becoming annoying. Yazmin liked her own space from time to time and Jai was starting to smother her. She pulled her car into a parking spot and hopped out to grab the groceries she was dropping off to her son. "What type of mother buys her grown ass sons groceries?" Jai muttered. "A good one," she said, as she grabbed the bags from the car. "I wonder how cocky you would be without that little job," Jai muttered. He didn't think Yazmin heard him, but she had heard him, loud and clear. She decided she would address it later. Yazmin's son ran out the apartment to help his mother when he saw her struggling to carry all the bags. "Ma, why you didn't call me to come out and help you?" he fussed, as he took the bags from her. Yazmin's son shook his head, as he looked over at Jai leaning against the car typing away on his phone. There was something about Jai her son didn't trust, and he would keep his guard up around him until he figured it out. Yazmin grabbed her son's mail out the mailbox along the wall, as she walked by. "When are they coming to fix the lock on your mailbox?" she asked, while flipping through his mail. Yazmin slipped his light bill in her purse, making a mental note to pay it the next day. "I'll try to remember tomorrow," Desmond told his mother as they walked into his apartment. Yazmin wanted to press the issue but decided to drop it. She didn't want to scold her son like a child in front of Jai. Yazmin could feel the tension in the room as she helped her son put up his groceries. She decided to cut her visit short and come back another day when she was alone. Yazmin gave her son a kiss and headed out the door, noticing Jai and her son never spoke two words.

Chapter 22

Yazmin rumbled around in her huge hobo purse trying to locate her ringing phone. When she finally pulled it out, she was surprised to see Terry's number flash across the screen. Yazmin hesitantly answered; she had not spoken to Terry since the day she moved out of their house. "Hey Yazmin, I was hoping you answered, I need to see you," Terry pleaded on the other end of the phone. The sound of Terry's voice pulled at Yazmin's heart, and she agreed to meet him that evening for dinner. As Yazmin nervously sat in the restaurant waiting for Terry to arrive, she wondered what he had to say. Terry entered the restaurant looking amazedly refreshed. The two sat in an awkward silence while waiting for the waiter to come and take their drink order. Yazmin's mouth dropped open in surprise when Terry ordered a glass of water, with a splash of lemon instead of his normal shot of whiskey. Terry noticed the shock look on Yazmin's face and smiled as he explained that he recently completed a twelve-week alcoholics anonymous course and had not drunk in months. Yazmin jumped up and ran around the table to and hug him, as he beamed with pride. "Wow Terry, you finally did it!", Yazmin gushed, while giving him a kiss on the cheek. As Yazmin sat back down a lady with the most angelic voice Yazmin had ever heard approached their table and begin to serenade them. Terry took both of Yazmin's hands into his and asked her for forgiveness for not being the type of husband she deserved and a chance to make it right. Yazmin was at a loss for words, their divorce would be final next week. She had waited so long to hear those magical words and as she starred into Terry's eyes, she realized the words she longed to hear for so long, had come too late. Yazmin still had love for Terry, but she was in love with Jai. He made her body feel things she had never imagined were possible. Terry knew her answer when she sat there silently. He waited until she stood and left the restaurant before he shed a few tears. Something in Yazmin's gut told her she was making a terrible decision, but she quickly dismissed those thoughts as Jai came to mind. The last few months of her life with him had been incredible. Jai's love kept her on a high, a high that helped ease the pain of losing her mother, and she wasn't ready to give that up.

As Yazmin walked out the courtroom with her official divorce papers, she couldn't shake the nagging feeling of regret in the pit of her stomach. She thought once her divorce was final, she would feel happy and carefree, instead she felt confused and scared. Yazmin ignored the constant ringing of her phone as she laid her head on the steering wheel and cried. She wasn't quite ready to go through with the divorce after having dinner with Terry the other night, but the constant pressure and accusations from Jai had started to become more than she could bear. Yazmin thought back to their last argument. *"What are you waiting for Yazmin!" Jai screamed while he paced the floor of their bedroom. "It's been long enough, I moved you into this lavish ass apartment, fully furnished it, take you on trips, and it's still not fuckin good enough! I thought you was different! I gave up all my hoes to be faithful to you!" he ranted. Yazmin sat quietly on the bed as she listened to him. Her heart was so torn. She couldn't help but to feel like she hadn't given her marriage a fair chance because she was so distracted by Jai. "I love you Yazmin! My mother is ill, I don't know how much longer she has to live, you're all I have," Jai cried, as he came and stood in front of her. Yazmin instantly felt bad; Jai had been her rock the entire time she grieved the loss of her mother. Now, here she was contemplating abandoning him in his time of need. Jai was an only child; besides a few neighborhood friends, his mother was all he had. His mother was now terminally ill, and doctors were unsure of how long she had left to live. Yazmin couldn't leave him at a time like this, she would be there for him, like he had been there for her. Yazmin reached for Jai and pulled him into an embrace. As she rubbed his back, she reassured him she wasn't going anywhere. When Jai saw his guilt trip was working, he knew now was the perfect time to go in for the kill. Jai dropped to his knees on the side of the bed and reached into his pocket to retrieve the 4 karat, princess cut, canary yellow, diamond engagement ring he had purchased for her. "I love you Yazmin, will you marry me?" he asked. Yazmin covered her mouth in shock, as Jai waited anxiously for her response. "This doesn't feel right," Yazmin thought. As she stared into Jai's pleading eyes, that were full of hope, she ignored every fiber in her body screaming, "Don't do it," and whispered, "Yes, baby I'll marry you!"* Yazmin pulled the beautiful ring out of her purse and slid it back on her finger. She had removed the ring from her finger before going into court that morning in fear of Terry noticing it. As she now sat in her car and looked at the beautiful ring, she knew it was too late to go back, and the only thing she could do is hope for the best moving forward. Yazmin sighed as she started her car and pulled off. She headed to the one place that always brought her peace, her parents' house.

Chapter 23

Yazmin could hear the low sound of gospel music playing as she entered her parent's house. She walked straight to the study room where she knew she would find her father reading his Bible. "Hey baby girl," he cheerly said, as Yazmin bent down and kissed him on the forehead. Yazmin was amazed by the day at her father's strength. Her parents had been married for forty years and she knew her father missed his wife terribly but still managed to be the glue that held the family together. No matter how busy Yazmin was, she always made time to come clean and cook for her father a few times a week. Jai would often complain about how much time she spent at her father's house but there was two things Yazmin would never compromise on, her father and her children. Nothing in this world was more important than family to her. "I'm going to make you spaghetti for dinner Daddy, that way you will have leftovers for tomorrow," she said as she turned to leave the room. "Yazmin Nicole Henderson sit down," he ordered. Yazmin knew her father had something serious on his mind because he never called her by her full name unless something was bothering him. Yazmin nervously sat back down on the couch, as she waited on her father to speak. "I am against what you are doing. You can't live in sin and expect God to bless you. This man you call yourself seeing means you no good!" "You don't even know him Daddy," Yazmin cried. "I don't have to know him, to know what my gut is telling me! You would hear what your gut is telling you as well if you open your ears and closed your legs," he spat. Yazmin was shocked, her father had never spoken to her in such a manner. Yazmin's father immediately felt bad after seeing the hurt look on his daughter's face and got up to go sit next to her. He wrapped his arms around her and wiped the tears from her face. "Young people nowadays are too quick to throw in the towel if something isn't going their way. Your mother and my marriage wasn't perfect, but we never gave up. If a man truly loves you, he will wait on you. Why all the rush? You are a nurturer by heart baby, but you always find the wrong people to nurture. Stop trying to fix everybody else and fix yourself. Open your eyes baby, before it's too late," he scolded. Yazmin sat in her father's arms and quietly listened to everything he had to say. She knew her father was right about a lot of things he was saying. That nagging feeling of regret was slowly returning. Every time she turned around; Yazmin found herself defending Jai. Her kids didn't like him, her family didn't like him, maybe she was in denial. "Stop chasing your body's desires and start chasing your soul's purpose," he sternly said. The two sat in silence for a few minutes as his words sunk in. Yazmin's father said a silent prayer over his daughter while she laid in his arms, his soul told him she would soon need it.

Jai couldn't be more relieved that Yazmin was now officially divorced. He knew she was contemplating giving her marriage another chance and if she and Terry stayed married, he worried she would go back to him. When the constant accusations of still being in love with Terry didn't work, Jai tried the next best thing, playing on Yazmin's conscience. Jai knew the guilt trips about her mother would work. Now he just needed to get her to the altar. Once they were married, he would have more control over her. But first he had to tie up one loose end. Jai pulled into the circular driveway of the home he shared with his wife and hopped out the car. He yelled his wife's name as he entered the house. Jai found her sitting at the kitchen table in the dark. "The stray dog has finally made his way home," she slurred. The house looked like it hadn't been cleaned in weeks and there was a half empty bottle of vodka sitting in front of her. Jai hadn't seen his wife in months. As long as she kept up her end of the bargain and kept his parole agent happy once a month, he would make sure all her bills were paid. Jai's wife knew better then to have another man in the house he paid for, she had witnessed up close and personal what he did to anybody who disrespected him. She still experienced occasional pain from the fractured jaw Jai had given her when she simply had a repair man in the house without prior permission from him. Jai threw the divorce papers on the table, "Sign," he coldly told her. Jai was prepared to break her jaw again if she tried to give him a hard time. Yazmin had no idea he was even married, and he planned to keep it that way. Jai wife swiped the papers onto the floor and laughed. "After all we been through nigga, you are divorcing me," she yelled. Her and Jai had been together for years. Yes, he treated her like shit, but she wasn't ready to give up the perks that came along with being the main woman in his life. The custom pearl white Lexus, her extensive fur collection and slew of diamonds, made her the instant envy of every bitch in the city. If only they knew about the frequent beatings that sent her to the hospital, being isolated from her family and friends, the outside kids, being pimped out for his convenience, and her husband's sick sex fetishes that included peeing on her, people probably wouldn't be so envious of her.

Chapter 24

Jai's wife knew her husband well. When he recently up and disappeared, she knew a new bitch had his attention. She heard through the grapevine, Jai was flossing some bitch around town, but just assumed it was another random hoe he added to his roster of women, that wouldn't be around for long. She didn't mind because it gave her a break from Jai's constant mental and physical abuse. Of course, she dibbled and dabbled a bit, what Jai didn't know wouldn't hurt him. "I'm not signing shit," she spat. Jai punched her so hard, her body flew across the table and bounced off the floor. Before she realized what happened, he closed in on her and punched her again. She tried to protect her face while Jai kicked and stomped all over her body. Just as she felt herself start to black out, Jai snatched her up by her hair and drug her back to the table. He grabbed the papers off the floor and placed them back in front of her. "Sign bitch! And you better not get a drop of blood on these papers," he growled. Her eyes were swelling so bad she could barely see the line to sign on. After she signed the papers, Jai loosened his grip on her hair as he leaned in and told her, "Don't change the locks, and you still have two more appointments with my parole agent you better not miss." When she didn't respond, Jai grabbed her head and slammed it on the table. "Bitch answer me," he yelled. She felt her front tooth crack when her face hit the table. "Yes, I understand," she whispered, scared for her life. When she heard the front door slam, she loudly sobbed, finally realizing nothing Jai gave her was more valuable than her life.

After a romantic stroll along the water, Yazmin and Jai decided to stop by and visit his mom. They could hear her laughing loudly as they entered the house.

"What's so funny Mama?" Jai asked, while giving her a kiss on the forehead. Regardless of how ruthless Jai was in the streets and to his women, he was always loving with his mother. "These silly late-night shows baby," she laughed.

"Hey Yazmin baby, come give Mama a hug." Yazmin leaned in to give Ms. Barbara a hug, making sure not to squeeze her too hard. She had lost a tremendous amount of weight since the last time Yazmin saw her. "How are you doing Mama Barbara?" she asked, while taking a seat on the couch next to her. "I would be much better if I had some chocolate ice cream," she said, cutting her eyes at her son. Jai already knew what that meant, she probably did want the ice cream, but she really wanted time to talk to Yazmin alone. Jai needed to call and check in on Harmony anyway. Mama Barbara grabbed Yazmin's hand once they were alone. "I want to thank you for being there for my son," she said as she began to cry. "I know he can be a bit much sometimes, but I know he loves you. He tells me all the time how you have made his life better, and he don't know what he would do without you. Promise me you will be there for him when I'm gone," she wept. Yazmin began to cry as well. She cried from the pain of losing her own mother, and the pain she knew Jai would soon have to endure. "I promise," she said.

Yazmin and Jai were married in a small chapel at the downtown courthouse one week later. Two months later Jai's mother passed. Jai was devasted. No matter what he did, right or wrong, his mother was always in his corner. The only woman he ever truly loved was now gone. Yazmin tried her best to be there for Jai like he had been there for her, but his constant accusations and verbal abuse was making it nearly impossible. Now that Yazmin was all Jai had, he became even more insecure. His constant fear of losing her made him suspicious of everything she did. He didn't trust her because he wasn't trustworthy himself.

Chapter 25

Yazmin stared in the full-length mirror admiring herself. Tonight, would be her first time meeting Jai's friends from his old neighborhood and he had given her strict instructions to be on point. After spending the entire day at the mall and hair salon, Yazmin was impressed with the results. Her wand curled hair beautifully framed her face, and her makeup as they say was, "Beat to the Gods," her pecan colored skin looked like it was actually glowing under the lights. Yazmin decided to be daring with her outfit since they were attending a party at one of the city's hottest strip clubs. The red lace corset she wore gave her breasts a full perky look, while the skin-tight high waist black jeans accented her bubble butt. She complimented the outfit with her spiked red bottom heels. Yazmin bent over and bounced her booty to the old-school hip-hop jam playing on the radio, "Girl you be killing em, you be killing 'em," she sang along with Fabolous. Jai walked in the room and was shocked by Yazmin's appearance. The new hairdo and make up she wore gave her a sexy and erotic look. The sexy outfit only added to her already sex appeal. Jai's dick instantly got hard just looking at her. Yazmin started to become uncomfortable under his stare and cleared her throat. "On point enough Daddy?" she teased, as she did a sexy twirl. "Just don't get fucked up tonight," he told her, as he roughly smacked her on the ass. Something in his tone told Yazmin he wasn't playing.

Jai held onto Yazmin tightly as the two made their way through the packed club. The loud music vibrated off the walls, as girls in all shapes and sizes walked around in jeweled G-strings. Men crowded around the stage, making it rain on a beautiful Asian looking stripper with the biggest ass Yazmin had ever seen. When they walked by the stage, Yazmin could have sworn she saw the stripper on stage give her a dirty look but quickly dismissed the thought. As her and Jai entered the VIP section, all eyes were on them. A few men were scattered throughout the area, while girls danced nude all around the room. Jai walked over and gave his boys a dap, then introduced Shotta to his girl. As Yazmin politely shook each guy's hand, the way Shotta gawked at her, made her feel slightly out of place. When the waitress came over and sat two bottles of champagne on their table, Yazmin couldn't be happier. She quickly downed two glasses of champagne to help loosen her up. As Yazmin sipped her third glass of champagne, she looked around the room and admired its classy décor. The one-way mirrors that lined the VIP area provided privacy from the rest of the club. A gold pole was centered in the middle of the floor, with three plush gold sofas surrounding it. A room for people to get private dances sat off to the right of the bar area. By the time midnight rolled around, Yazmin was buzzing and relaxed. Jai and his friends were on their third bottle of patron feeling good. The men had thrown so much money at the dancers you could hardly see the floor. Yazmin went over to where Jai was sitting and straddled him. Jai grabbed her ass as she grinded on him. They were so into their own world; they didn't notice someone standing over them until Yazmin felt a light tap on the shoulder. She spun around and was face to face with the beautiful stripper from on stage.

Harmony couldn't believe Jai had the nerve to bring this bitch in her job and embarrass her like that. He walked right past her like she was a piece of trash. By the way he held the woman's hand protectively and walked her through the club, this had to be his precious Yazmin.

Harmony had never been a hater, so she had to admit Yazmin was definitely competition. She was pretty, had a nice little shape, and Harmony could tell she carried herself like a boss. After seeing her, Harmony knew no matter how hard she tried, Jai would never leave Yazmin for her. Harmony was just convenient pussy for him. Jai couldn't floss Harmony around his friends as his woman when just about every one of them had saw her body for just a few dollars. The more Harmony thought about everything, the clearer it all became. Jai didn't love her or Yazmin, he only loved himself. Harmony was finally ready to see shit for what it was and move on. But not before giving Jai a little dose of his own medicine. Harmony walked out of the dressing room and headed straight to the VIP area. As the club's number one dancer she knew she wouldn't have any trouble gaining access to the exclusive area. When Harmony entered the room, she immediately spotted the love birds lost in their own world. Jai was groping on Yazmin's fat ass, while she slowly grinded and rotated her hips in his lap. Harmony knew in her heart she was over the entire situation when she found the scene more arousing then upsetting. She strolled over and tapped Yazmin on her shoulder, when she turned around, Harmony noticed she was even prettier up close. Harmony could see Jai's body tense up, unsure of what to expect. Harmony offered to give Yazmin a private lap dance and was shocked at how easily she agreed. Harmony grabbed a bottle of champagne off the table and led Yazmin to the private dance area toward the back of the room. She licked her lips and blew Jai a kiss as they brushed past him. She was ready to put on her show.

Chapter 26

Harmony pushed her breasts in Yazmin's face as she gyrated in her lap. She took delight in the look of discomfort on Jai's face as he watched them from across the room. Jai knew better than to make a scene and arouse Yazmin's suspicions, but he would definitely make sure Harmony's ass paid for this little stunt later. Yazmin was so memorized by the feel of Harmony's body all over hers, she didn't notice the little blue pill Harmony slipped in the champagne bottle she was sipping on. Over the next two songs, Harmony and Yazmin sipped from the champagne bottle while groping and feeling all over each other. When Harmony felt Yazmin's hand glide over her crotch area, she knew the effects of the pill had started to kick in. Harmony rocked back and forth on Yazmin's hand, enjoying the sensation she was giving her. Yazmin took her thumb and rubbed it across Harmony's clit while using her middle finger to find her g-spot. When Yazmin felt Harmony's body tense up she sped up her pace. As the two stared into each other's eyes, Harmony held her breath to stop from screaming out loud, as an orgasm took over her body. Harmony continued to dance on Yazmin, as her juices flowed down Yazmin's hand. Jai was no longer enjoying himself and was ready for everybody to leave. The men were completely ignoring the dancers and focused on Yazmin and Harmony making out in the back of the room. Harmony was now completely naked, pushing her perky titties in Yazmin's face, while she bounced up and down in her lap. Jai ushered the gawking men out of the room and over to the bar to settle their tab. He grabbed the attention of a security guard, slipped him a hundred-dollar bill and instructed him to not let anyone in the room until he got back. Ten minutes later, Jai sprinted across the bar, back to the room, hoping that bitch Harmony hadn't said the wrong thing to Yazmin. Jai nearly knocked the security guard down trying to get back in the room. What he saw when he entered the room, stopped him dead in his tracks. Yazmin was laid back on the couch with Harmony's head buried deep between her legs. Jai had always fantasized about a threesome with the two of them, but it was something he wanted to initiate, to be in control. He felt the bulge in his pants grow as he watched Harmony sucking and slurping on Yazmin's gushiness. When Harmony noticed Jai watching them out the corner of her eye, she bounced her ass and made it clap a few times, knowing it would draw him in. Just as she thought, Jai's anger was quickly replaced with lust at the sight of Harmony's ass in the air, with her head bobbing and weaving between Yazmin's legs. In one swift motion, Jai crossed the room, dropped his jeans and slid in Harmony from behind, while she had Yazmin squealing in pure delight. Although she had never feasted on another woman's sweetness before today, the ecstasy pill made her feel like a pro. Harmony flicked her tongue across Yazmin's clit while massaging her g-spot. Jai couldn't help but to feel a little jealous at seeing someone else please his wife more than him. Acting on his insecurities he pulled one of Yazmin's legs toward him and begin to suck on her toes. When Harmony saw this, she became consumed with jealousy. While still massaging Yazmin's clit with her finger, Harmony arched her back and begin to throw her ass in a circle. When she felt Jai speed up his strokes, she rotated her ass faster to match his rhythm. "You like that baby?" she sexily asked. "Yes," he grunted. Harmony was dripping wet from the ecstasy pills she'd consumed. The sight of Harmony's round ass swaying back and forth had Jai fighting not to cum prematurely. Harmony reached her free hand under her and gently massaged Jai's balls. He threw his head back to fight off the urge of screaming out like a bitch! Just when she knew Jai was right where she wanted him, Harmony seductively looked back at Jai, and asked him was this the best pussy he ever had, making sure Yazmin was listening. If Harmony couldn't be happy, she was going to make sure Yazmin and Jai wasn't happy either. Harmony held her breath while she waited on Jai reply. The large amount of liquor Jai had consumed all the night didn't have him thinking clearly, when he groaned yes Harmony smiled while looking Yazmin in the eyes. Harmony expected her to jump up mad, cursing Jai out, instead she grabbed Harmony's head and shoved it back between her legs. "Do something useful with that mouth," Yazmin barked. She wasn't a fool, Yazmin could tell by how in tune Jai and Harmony's body was, this wasn't their first time being together. If Jai was having his fun, she would too. Harmony didn't mind playing along because she had already got what she wanted, causing a problem in Jai's little "perfect relationship." She pushed Yazmin's legs back as far as they would go and slid her tongue back in her. Harmony reached up and played with Yazmin's nipples while she feasted on her sweetness. Before long Yazmin's legs began to quiver, letting Harmony know she was about to cum. Harmony felt Yazmin grab her head, as Jai roughly smacked her on the ass. Jai and Yazmin both groaned in pleasure, as they came at the same time. Harmony suddenly no longer felt like she had won. As she laid there filled with both Yazmin and Jai's cum, she felt used and dirty. Jai threw a wad of money on top of her, grabbed Yazmin around the waist and left out the room.

Chapter 27

Yazmin awoke to Jai roughly shaking her. "What's wrong baby?" she asked still half asleep. "Are you gay?" he asked bluntly. Yazmin opened her eyes fully and looked at him like he had suddenly grew two heads. When she saw Jai was serious, she fell back laughing. "You can't be fuckin' serious right now," she managed to say, after getting herself together. Jai didn't find one thing funny. He had noticed how comfortable Yazmin was with Harmony between her legs. This definitely wasn't her first time with a woman. "Bitch do I look like I'm laughing?" he asked in a tone Yazmin had never heard him use before. "Bitch do I look like I care," she snapped back. No one had ever talked to Jai like that before in his life. It was time he showed Yazmin who the boss was. Yazmin hopped out the bed and went into the kitchen to grab a bottle of water. She couldn't believe Jai had woken her up out of her sleep with such foolishness. She leaned against the refrigerator sipping her water, as Jai walked into the kitchen ranting and raving. "Did you like how she licked your pussy?" he asked in a childish tone. "You were enjoying yourself so much you forgot I was even in the room!" Yazmin glared at him before responding, "I didn't forget, I just didn't care!" Yazmin stormed into the bedroom, slammed and locked the bedroom door. Jai was enraged as he kicked on the door. "Open this door bitch," he screamed. Jai kicked the door so hard it flew off the hinges, and he found himself looking straight down the barrel of Yazmin's 9mm pistol. She calmly tossed him a few sheets of paper. Jai's heart sunk as his eyes scanned the printed screenshots fluttering around the room. Right there, in black and white, were direct message sent through Facebook from Harmony to Yazmin, giving her full details of their relationship. Jai stood there stunned. "I can see why you like her," Yazmin laughed, while licking her lips. "Get out," she calmly said, with her gun still trained on him. Jai had no other choice but to leave. He jumped in his car and headed straight to Harmony's house, all the while trying to figure out the most painful way, he could make her pay.

Jai was so anxious to get his hands on Harmony, he jumped out of his car and left in running. Her apartment was pitch black as he entered. When Jai hit the light switch, he was completely shocked that her apartment was empty. He went from room to room, searching for anything that would tell him where she could have gone, but came up with nothing. Then a light switch went off in his head, her mother. If he couldn't get to Harmony, he would use the next best thing. As Jai raced back to the front of the apartment, he noticed a piece of paper taped to the door. He had been in such a rage when he first entered the apartment, he had completely missed the sheet of paper. Jai snatched the paper down and read it. It was Harmony's mother obituary, who had died several weeks ago. Harmony had written the words; *Now You See How It Feels to Get Fucked Over!* in bold red letters across the top of the paper. Jai balled up the obituary feeling something he had never felt before, defeated. The way he mistreated people over the years was finally starting to catch up with him. Whether he wanted to admit it or not, he actually loved Yazmin. For the first time in his life he had found a woman that completed him. He didn't know why he cheated when he had something so special at home.

Chapter 28

Yazmin threw her stuff in her locker in the break room and rushed to her desk. She was hoping Megan was too busy to notice she was a few minutes late. Before Yazmin could sit down and cut on her computer, Megan called her into the office. Over the past few months, Megan had noticed a change in Yazmin. Where Yazmin was once the office star employee, being on time every day, outgoing and patient with customers, she now rushed into work at the very last minute and always seemed distracted and distant. At first, Megan contributed the change in Yazmin's behavior to the passing of her mother. However, after noticing Yazmin sitting in her car during her lunch break a few times with a man other than Terry, Megan knew it was something more going on. She tried not to get in her co-workers' business, but she didn't want to see Yazmin ruin everything she had worked so hard for. Yazmin had potential to go far with the bank and Megan prayed she wouldn't let a man ruin it. Something about this new man in Yazmin's life just didn't sit well with her. Megan shook her head as Yazmin took a seat across from her. "What's going on with you Yazmin?" she asked disapprovingly.

Yazmin stared at the floor as she thought about her response. Between her mother's death, her divorce, the boutique and the constant arguing with Jai, she was stressed out. Everything was just becoming too much, and she knew her job was suffering because of it. "I'm sorry Megan," she cried. "I'm just under a lot of stress right now." Megan came from around the desk and pulled Yazmin into a tight hug. "You are a bright woman Yazmin, don't let anyone dim your light," she sadly sad. Yazmin promised Megan she would do better. She had to find a way to get rid of some of the stress in her life, even if it meant getting rid of Jai.

Jai was relentless in trying to get his wife back. He moved into his mother's old house to respect her space. Jai would text Yazmin all day telling her how much he loved and missed her with no response back. The flowers he sent were all refused and marked return to sender. He would drive by her apartment at night to make sure her car was home, and she wasn't out entertaining another nigga. Jai missed Yazmin something terrible and vowed to do right by her if he ever got her back. He decided to make one last effort before giving up all hope. Jai picked up the dozen custom made purple roses he ordered, along with Yazmin's favorite meal from Red Lobster, and sat outside her job and waited. When Jai saw her exiting the building at five p.m., he hopped out of his car and slowly approached her. Yazmin tried her best to ignore him as she made her way to her vehicle, but he looked so pitiful her heart went out to him. "What do you want Jai?" she asked in frustrated tone. "Just five minutes of your time please," he begged. Yazmin hit the unlock button on her car as they both got in. She snatched the Red Lobster bag from his lap and opened the carry out, might as well put something on my stomach while listening to his bullshit, she figured. Yazmin almost choked on a piece of shrimp when Jai admitted he had cheated on her with Harmony. She was expecting to hear a bunch of lies but Jai actually sounded sincere. Yazmin couldn't help but to feel bad when Jai talked about how lonely he was without her and his mother. She wasn't ready to forgive Jai, but she wasn't ready to divorce him either. Deep down, she was too embarrassed to admit to everyone she had made a mistake divorcing Terry and marrying Jai. "You throw in the towel too quick," her father voice played back in her head. When in reality some people should have never been handed the towel in the first place.

Chapter 29

Jai was on his best behavior trying to win Yazmin back. While she didn't allow him to come over, they would meet up for dates and talk on the phone for hours at night like when they first met. Jai wasn't perfect but Yazmin gave him credit for trying. No one knew the two of them were separated, so Jai hoped Yazmin would still attend his little cousin's birthday party with him in a few days and was thrilled when she agreed to go. Jai pulled up to Yazmin's apartment and blew the horn, hoping one day soon, he would be allowed back inside. Yazmin got in the car and gave Jai a light peck on the lips. When she turned to buckle her seat belt, she noticed a small teddy bear sitting on the back seat with a silver bracelet dangling around its neck sitting on the back seat. Pulling the bracelet off the bear, she saw her boutique named inscribed on the inside. Snapping the bracelet around her wrist, Yazmin leaned in and the two shared a passionate kiss. "Maybe I'll give you a little reward tonight," she winked. Jai was thankful his cousin's party was at the arcade right up the street, he was anxious to get back and get some of Yazmin's loving. He was so distracted by their separation; he had not bothered sleeping with anyone else.

Jai and Yazmin could have easily been mistaken for two teenagers on their first date. They ran around the arcade and competed in everything from air hockey to basketball. By the time the two were ready to leave, they were both wore out. As they headed toward the exit, hand in hand, Yazmin spotted a familiar face. Nadia, she screamed as she ran toward her old friend. The two women shared a warm hug while breaking their embrace. Nadia noticed the huge rock on Yazmin's finger. "Upgraded the ring," she beamed. "And the man," Yazmin laughed. "Come meet my husband," she said, dragging Nadia over to Jai. "What the fuck!" Nadia yelled so loud;

people turned around to look at them. Yazmin stood there dumbfounded as Nadia pointed her finger in Jai face. "This the bitch you left me for?" Yazmin looked back and forth between the two of them. "Wait! What?" Yazmin yelled. "Jai has never been married," she stuttered. "And I thought your husband's name was Dre?" Yazmin was asking a million questions all at once. "It is!" Nadia yelled, Jai'andre." As reality started to set in, Yazmin began to feel lightheaded. Her Jai was Nadia's husband Dre. "Jai'andre," both women said at the same time. The same Dre Yazmin had heard so many awful stories about. How could this even be possible. How could he have been married for most of their relationship when he spent so much time with her? Yazmin knew the only person who could answer those questions was Nadia. She turned and smacked Jai as hard as she could, before running out the arcade.

Yazmin nervously bounced her leg up and down on the barstool, as she sat at the bar and waited for Nadia to arrive. She was still in complete shock. "It's a small world after all," she muttered to herself, while downing her peach Long Island. She signaled for the bartender to bring her another one, just as Nadia walked in. The sat in an awkward silence while the two waited for their drinks. "I swear I didn't know," Yazmin was the first to say. Nadia had thought long and hard about the situation over the last few days. Honestly, there was no reason for Yazmin to suspect Jai was married. He didn't behave like a married man. He would leave home for months at a time, daring anyone, even his wife, to question his whereabouts. Jai made more than enough money to lavish all of his women with comfortable life styles. Most married men wouldn't dare be caught in public with another woman, not Jai. He didn't care who saw him. If they went back and told his wife, what was she going to do? "I believe you," Nadia sadly sad. The two women sat and compared notes over the next two hours. Yazmin was ashamed to say the least. Here she was married to a man she hardly even knew. Nadia and Jai had only been divorced one month before her and Jai were married, which meant he had a wife she knew nothing about their entire relationship. Yazmin had been honest with Jai from the jump concerning her and Terry's situation, but he hadn't returned the favor. "Hold on," Yazmin suddenly said. I thought I remember you saying Dre has a son. "He does," Nadia said. "That's whose party I saw you guys at the other day. You didn't know?" Yazmin was completely floored. That sick bastard. Jai had the nerve to have her sitting at his son's birthday party pretending it was his little cousin the entire time it was his damn son. And what was even more fucked up was the fact that his baby mother had sat there and played right along. Yazmin was filing for an annulment first thing tomorrow morning. Fuck what everybody thought! She was ready to admit she had fucked up. Big time!

Chapter 30

"Who the fuck is banging on my door this damn early," Jai yelled, as he yanked the door open. "Are you Jai'andre?" the short, stocky man firmly asked. "Who the fuck wants to know?" "You've been served," the man rudely said, shoving an envelope into Jai's hands. Jai slammed the door shut and ripped open the envelope. This bitch really went and filed for a divorce he chuckled. Jai tore the papers in half and went back to sipping on his bottle of liquor. He had been in a drunken stupor since the other day. Just when he finally tried to do right, all his lies had finally caught up with him. He tried to contact Yazmin several times, but she had changed her number. Jai went by her apartment only to find she had packed all her stuff and moved out. He was so desperate that he went to Yazmin's job hoping to see her, only to have her manager rudely tell him she was on an indefinite leave of absence. The longer Jai went without talking to Yazmin, the angrier he became. After all he had done for the ungrateful bitch, she had the nerve to up and leave him. So fuckin' what he cheated, every man cheats. He had cheated on every bitch he was ever with and they had never left him. "I'll show this bitch who she fuckin with," Jai fumed. He was blaming everyone else for his mistakes except the person who was to blame, himself. Jai knew eventually Yazmin would go back to work, so every afternoon he rode past her job looking for her car. He was ecstatic when he finally spotted it a week later. Jai marched in the door and approached Yazmin's counter. He didn't care that she was with a customer, he shoved the elderly man out the way and demanded his wife speak to him." Are you crazy?" Yazmin shrieked. When Jai noticed Yazmin wasn't wearing her wedding ring, he lost it. "Bitch you leaving me?" he loudly screamed, causing everyone in the bank to look at him. Megan rushed from out of her office and stood directly behind Yazmin. "Sir,

I'm going to have to ask you to leave before I call the police," she boldly told him. Jai was fuming. "I'll ruin your life bitch before I let you walk out of mine," he snarled. Jai knocked over a stack of papers, before walking out the building. Yazmin decided to file a personal protection order against Jai after seeing him repeatedly sitting in the back of her job watching her all week. After her job found out Jai was on parole, they wanted her to write a statement and press formal charges against him, but she refused, Yazmin just wanted to divorce Jai and forget this nightmare had ever happened. She wasn't from the streets, but she was well aware of the dangers that came along with being labeled a "snitch." After taking another week off work, Yazmin had calmed down enough to return to work. Her day was going smoothly, with no signs of Jai popping up and stalking her. She was praying once he was served with the personal protection order he would finally get through his head their marriage was over and nothing he said or did would change that. Yazmin hadn't spoken to Nadia since their meeting the other day. Although Nadia claimed to understand the situation, Yazmin still had a feeling she was feeling some type of way about her. After all, whether Yazmin knew Jai was married or not, in the end, he had still divorced Nadia to marry her. She swore to Nadia she would never mention their relationship to Jai. Just as Yazmin was headed out for lunch, Megan asked her to step inside her office. An uneasy feeling filled Yazmin's body, as she stepped into Megan's office and noticed the region manager and HR personnel sitting behind Megan's desk. "Have a seat, Yazmin," the region manager sternly said. As Yazmin took a seat, she glanced over at Megan. She could tell Megan was unsure of what was going on, but they both knew with HR being involved, it couldn't be anything good. Yazmin's heart thumped in her chest as the HR rep leaned back in her chair, folded her arms and coldly told her, "Unfortunately Ms. Henderson, we are suspending you pending an investigation based on allegations of fraud." It took a minute for Yazmin's mind to register what her ears had just heard. When everything finally clicked, she jumped from her seat in shock. "Fraud!" she yelled. "Are you serious? I would never do anything to risk my job," she fumed. Megan looked on sympathetically as the region manager grabbed Yazmin by the arm and escorted her off the premises. Yazmin couldn't stop the tears from falling down her face as she sat in her car frozen in complete and utter shock. She couldn't believe this was happening to her. Who would accuse her of fraud, she wondered out loud. "That bitch," Yazmin screamed. Nadia had to be behind this. She had means and a motive. She was a bitter and jealous bitch. After all Jai had put her dumb ass through, she was still upset over losing him. Yazmin bailed out of the parking lot at a high rate of speed, headed to see the one person who could fix this.

Chapter 31

Yazmin stormed onto Jai's porch and kicked the door as hard as she could. "Open the door fuck nigga," she screamed. Jai snatched the door open so hard; the frame shook. "Call your lying ass ex-wife right now!" When Jai didn't move, Yazmin pushed past him and barged into the house. As she stood in the middle of the living room, with her arms folded and nostril flaring, Jai just stared at her. Yazmin looked even more beautiful when she was mad. "Calm down Yazmin and tell me what happened," Jai's calmness was pissing Yazmin off. "Your lying ass ex-wife called my job and reported me for fraud. Now I'm suspended from work while they investigate me," she fumed. Yazmin sat on the couch sobbing, as everything started to hit her all at once. She had been a model employee for years and was devastated at the thought of losing her job. She just prayed this HR investigation proved she had never done anything fraudulently during her employment. Jai sat down on the couch next to Yazmin and rubbed her back. He tried to find the right words to sooth her. "Baby, Nadia wouldn't do anything like that. She knows what I would do if I ever found out she was behind something like that," he said. Yazmin thought about what Jai was saying and had to admit it was some truth to his statement. After suffering years of physical abuse, Nadia never hid her fear of Jai. When Jai saw Yazmin was contemplating what he was saying, he continued, "Your job is just trying to get under your skin because you didn't press charges on me, like they wanted you to. You have done nothing wrong, and when they discover that, you will be back to work in no time," he finished. Yazmin thought long and hard about what Jai was saying. What he said made a lot of sense. Her job was extremely upset when she refused to press assault charges against Jai. In her heart, she knew she had done nothing wrong, so she started to feel a little better about the situation. "Yazmin, we need to talk," Jai pleaded. "Jai this changes nothing. Our whole marriage was built on a lie, it over." She couldn't believe Jai actually thought there was a chance in hell of them reconciling after all the lies he had told. "It's over when I say it's over," Jai challenged. Yazmin shook her head while walking out the door. Just that fast Jai's evilness had popped up, reminding her he was a wolf in sheep's clothing.

While on suspension Yazmin threw herself into her store. Because she always worked full time, Yazmin never had an abundance of time to dedicate solely to growing her business. With the free time she now had, she devoted herself to creating new ways to market and advertise her boutique. Yazmin was so wrapped up in her business, before she knew it, she had been off work for six months. Although she missed her co-workers dearly, the break from the everyday hustle and bustle of a nine to five was appreciated. As Yazmin got ready to leave home for the day, she could hear her youngest son up fixing breakfast in the kitchen before leaving out for his morning classes. Yazmin couldn't have been more thrilled to have her kids coming back over on a regular basis. The entire time she was with Jai, Yazmin had to go visit her kids at their home because they refused to step foot in the home her and Jai shared. Her kids never trusted him and would not pretend like they did. Yazmin walked in the kitchen and snatched a piece of bacon off her son's plate. "Ma, it's a whole plate of bacon on the counter," he laughed. "I know, but I want yours," Yazmin said, lightly smacking him in the back of the head. The sudden pounding on the front door, caused them both to pause. Yazmin lightly jogged to the door, determined to see what could possibly be so urgent this early in the morning. "Police, open up!" was yelled out, just as Yazmin reached for the door handle. Before she could fully open the door, police in full swat uniforms stormed her house. Yazmin panicked and yelled out to the officers her son was in the house. She didn't know what was going on, but she didn't want her son shot and killed in the process of trying to find out. As Yazmin was placed in handcuffs and walked outside, she breathed a sigh of relief when they brought her son out a few minutes later. She tried to stay calm, but her heart was nearly beating out of her chest. All of her neighbors had begun to hurdle outside, to witness what looked like a movie scene.

Chapter 32

The crackling of the detective's walkie - talkie in the front seat of the police cruiser caught Yazmin's attention. "Second location secured!" What second location she wondered. It didn't take long before she found out. The detective held up a piece of paper in front of her that read search warrant with her address on it. When he held up the second warrant, she was unfamiliar with the address. When the detective noticed her confusion, he chuckled. "Playing dumb, are we? Please don't act like you don't recognize your own son's address," he said. Yazmin couldn't recite her son's address from memory if her life depended on it. He had only lived there a few months and the apartment complex he lived in was huge. She was only able to find his particular building by landmarks in the parking lot. Addresses were nothing more than a bunch of numbers to her, it was much easier for her to use landmarks instead.

Yazmin prayed her son was fully cooperating with the police and wasn't giving them any reason to hurt him. Her wrist began to feel numb from the handcuffs being on so tight. She had never been placed in handcuffs before a day in her life. As the officers carried large paper bags from her home, she was curious to know what was in them. "You better hope we don't find any printing machines or water marked paper in you or your son's home," the officer chuckled from the front seat. Yazmin now figured this all had something to do with her job, as she sat quietly in the back of the police cruiser. She felt a lot of emotions as the cruiser pulled off headed to the police station and regret was the biggest one of them. In the blink of an eye, her life had gone from sugar to shit. She went from living in her dream home to now facing the possibility of living in a jail cell and had no one to blame but herself!

"Yazmin Henderson!" the burly white woman said, as she sat down and placed a folder in front of her. Yazmin chose to remain quiet while she tried to figure out her situation. She had learned from watching enough criminal shows that the more a person said, the bigger hole they dug for themselves. "Do you know why you are here, Ms. Henderson?" When the detective saw Yazmin wasn't going to respond she continued. "You are being charged with ten felonies." Yazmin swallowed the bile taste that was rising from the pit of her stomach. She felt like she would throw up any minute. "Do you remember cashing these checks," the detective asked. Yazmin glanced down at the paper and squinted to get a better look. She cashed hundreds, if not thousands of checks every week. They all looked the same. Yazmin didn't know if the detective was trying to trick her or not, so she remained quiet. "Just admit to me why you did this, and we will work out a deal for you." Yazmin shook her head and laughed at the Doctor Jekyll and Mr. Hyde impersonation the detective was putting on. "Did your husband coerce you into doing this?" the detective asked. Yazmin frowned at the mention of Jai's name. *What did he have to do with this* she wondered. When the detective noticed Yazmin's discomfort, she began to lay more papers down on the table. "Were you aware of your husband's lengthy criminal record and even lengthier list of women?" she smirked. As hard as Yazmin tried, she couldn't stop the tears from rolling down her face as she slowly looked over the pictures. Jai and Harmony sitting outside under a picnic table, looking like a happy family, with an older lady, at what looked to be some sort of rehabilitation center. Jai and the son Yazmin never even knew existed, walking hand in hand with Kam, the child's mother through Disneyland. They even had pictures of Jai and Nadia enjoying a cozy dinner at her and Jai's favorite restaurant. The dates in the corner of each picture confirmed all the photos were taken during her and Jai's relationship. She shook her head in disbelief, Jai had been living a complete double life since the day she met him.

Yazmin had been foolish enough to throw in the towel on her marriage with Terry for someone she didn't even know. Sometimes the grass looks greener on the other side because that shit is fake!

Chapter 33

Over the next several hours, different detectives took turns badgering Yazmin about her and Jai's relationship. The detectives were confident Yazmin knew more then what she was saying. They had one more trick up their sleeves to try to get her to talk. Yazmin groaned in frustration when the burly female detective stepped back in the room. She had been there for hours trying to convince them she was innocent of what they were accusing her of.

She was tired, upset, and worried about her children because she knew they were worried sick about her. "Ms. Henderson do you know what a discovery pack is?" the detective asked. She scooted her chair closer to the table. "A discovery pack is a packet put together by investigating officers over your case. This here," she paused as she held up a thick stack of papers, "is your discovery pack Ms. Henderson. The first page normally describes the basis of an investigation including why it was started." The detective flipped to the first page and placed the stack of papers at an angle where they both could read them. "Read line four for me," the detective calmly told her. Yazmin scanned to line four and her blood instantly began to boil.

Incident Report - Region Manager Todd Jenkins was contacted by Branch Manager Megan Davis concerning a domestic incident that occurred within her branch. One of her employees was being harassed by an unknown suspect at her work counter. Mr. Jenkins instructed the branch manager to contact the police and that he should be arriving to the office shortly thereafter. After discovering the suspect in the office was in fact Yazmin Henderson's husband, a police report was filled out by office security personnel. Later that afternoon, a call was placed to Internal Affairs concerning allegations of fraud made against Yazmin Henderson. The caller stated Yazmin Henderson has been deliberately cashing fraudulent checks at her job. When asked how the caller knew this information, he stated, "Because I'm her husband."

"Bullshit!" Yazmin screamed. Jai may be a lying, cheating asshole, but he is not a snitch, he lived by the street code. He would never do no shit like this. The detective calmly pulled out a tape recorder and placed it on the desk and pushed the play button. Yazmin dropped her head in hurt, disappointment, and rage, as she listened to the recording. Because she worked at a financial institution, all phone calls were recorded. There was absolutely no denying the fact the voice of the caller making the allegations against Yazmin coming through the tape recorder was Jai's distinctive voice. "He didn't marry you because he loved you sweetie. He rushed to marry you to protect himself. Your husband used a fake ID to cash those checks. The only person who can testify to that is you. However, being that you are now his wife, you can't do that under spousal privilege. Which leaves you holding the bag," she smirked. "Do yourself a favor and help us. Can you tell us anything about your husband's criminal activity?" she said sliding a pen and paper across the table to Yazmin. If they thought they were going to get any sort of formal statement from Yazmin, they were sadly mistaken. "I want a lawyer," Yazmin coldly stated as she stared off into space. The detective actually started to feel bad for the naive girl. It was obvious her husband had preyed on her naivete, just as her father had predicted.

Yazmin couldn't be more thrilled when she heard the officer call her name to be released. Although she had only been in the holding cell for a few hours, with all the information she was just given to digest, it felt like years. How could Jai do this to her? All she had ever tried to do was love him. Who could be so sick and evil to try and destroy a person that had only tried to help them? Yazmin had not asked for a penny from Jai when she filed for divorce. She didn't want his money or any parts of his businesses, businesses that she helped him build. Why would he do this? Yazmin went back and forth between sadness and rage as she thought about everything. The one feeling that stuck with her more than anything, was the regret of not listening to her gut. She now realized that nagging voice in her head and in the pit of her stomach that kept trying to warn her over and over again, was God trying to send her red flags. Flags she probably would not have missed if she wasn't so busy chasing lust instead of peace.

Jai would pay, but first she had to prove her innocence. Yazmin's kids didn't give her time to descend the stairs as she stepped out of the police station, before they raced to her. "What the hell is going on Ma?" her older son asked. Yazmin filled her sons in on everything, as they drove her home. She felt like crying all over again once she entered her apartment. The police had completely ransacked everything. Clothes and papers were everywhere. "Don't feel bad Ma, my apartment looks the same way," her son said. In the midst of everything, Yazmin had almost forgotten her son's apartment had been raided as well, because it was in her name. "I'm so sorry baby," she cried as she grabbed her kids in for a hug. Yazmin jumped on the phone and scheduled an appointment with her attorney for the next morning, while her sons began to clean up the apartment. Things were getting more out of control by the minute.

Chapter 34

Yazmin put on her game face as she sat across from her lawyer. Attorney Shaw was one of the top lawyers in Detroit. He came at a pretty hefty penny, but Yazmin's father insisted his baby girl have the best lawyer money could buy. As her attorney flipped through her paperwork, Yazmin admired the office deep mahogany décor. Every wall in the room was covered with plaques and degrees Attorney Shaw had received over the years. She shifted her attention back to him when he began to shuffle papers around. "How bad is it?" she nervously asked. "Well it seems that your husband's accusation of fraudulent activity against you, prompted an investigation to be started by internal affairs. They went through all of your transactions over the last seven years and found two fraudulent checks you cashed a few months ago." "What?" Yazmin asked flabbergasted. She would never knowingly cash a fraudulent check on her job. "Is it possible it was a mistake?" she cried. "If the check was professionally constructed, it could have just slipped past me! It happens all the time." Yazmin was outdone. "Well your job probably would have took all that into consideration, had your husband not insinuated that you intentionally cashed fraudulent checks for financial gain. And it certainly doesn't help that he was in fact the person who came in and cashed the checks," Attorney Shaw added, in his sharp lawyer tone. Yazmin sat there in shock, as flashbacks began to hit her. She thought about Jai coming into her job, cashing two checks, around the time they first met. Any other time she would have paid more attention to the checks before cashing them, but just as Jai planned, she was so distracted by his charm, she hadn't given the checks a second look. Jai's words played over and over in Yazmin's head. *"Bitch, I'll ruin your life before I let you walk out of mine."* Now Yazmin wished she would have believed him. All it took was one false allegation from a scorned man to have her now facing the rest of her life behind bars. The job she had dedicated her life to for years had not even tried to get her side of the story before prosecuting her. If they had, they would know all she was trying to do was get out of a toxic relationship that was slowly destroying her. As Yazmin sat in the office and cried, Attorney Shaw couldn't help but to feel bad for the young woman. When he first took on her case, he initially felt like she was guilty. But after reading over everything and getting Yazmin's side of the story, he now felt different, and would try his best to prove it. "With help on your part, I'm sure we can win," Attorney Shaw confidently said. He made a list of all the information he would need from Yazmin. Yazmin was anxious to leave and get started. Getting revenge was the last thing on her mind right now. Maybe this was her karma for marrying Jai in the first place. She had been so blinded by lust; she had lost herself somewhere along the way.

Jai paced around his office in the detail shop, occasionally glancing at the cameras, which showed various angles of the shop. Normally Jai would be thrilled to see the lobby packed with customers, but his mind was somewhere else today. He looked around the office in sadness, as he admired the way Yazmin had decorated it for him. He cringed every time he thought about what he had done. *Jai was livid as he stormed out of Yazmin's job. The feeling of rejection was unfamiliar to him and he didn't like how it felt one bit. This was all her father's fault for putting that bitch on a pedestal all these years. Now with her little job and boutique she thought she was better than everybody else. Jai should have demanded she quit that fuckin' job months ago. He needed his bitch to depend on him to maintain control in the relationship. No matter how bad he treated all his bitches, they always came back for one reason, the money. Harmony needed him to pay for her* mother's medical expenses and Nadia needed his money to maintain her luxurious lifestyle. He dangled the power of money in front of everyone in his life as a way to use, abuse and mistreat them, and up until now, it had worked. Suddenly a thought popped into his head. *I bet that bitch will need me if she no longer has that little job*, he mischievously laughed. The shots of Patron didn't have him thinking clearly as he googled the number to Yazmin's job's headquarters. Jai was so engulfed in his own twisted rage, he was moving out of pure emotions. If he had been in his right mind, Jai would have realized the call he was making to falsely accuse Yazmin of a crime, would implicate him of a crime as well, after all, he had been the one to come in and actually cash the checks. Yazmin was completely unaware the checks were fraudulent. He just hoped this was not something she could prove. Jai had no intentions of starting a massive investigation that would lead to criminal charges being filed against Yazmin. He only intended to get her fired from her job, in hopes that she would come crawling back to him, because she needed him. The day Yazmin showed up at his house accusing Nadia of being the person who called her job, Jai nearly jumped for joy when he realized Yazmin did not suspect him. He figured they would be back together in no time. What he hadn't anticipated was Yazmin's income at the boutique nearly doubling, now that she didn't need to pay part time help and could invest more time in her business. When Jai heard through the streets Yazmin was opening up a social club he felt completely defeated and regretted what he had done. It didn't matter if Yazmin had that job or not, he now understood she was a different type of woman and would be okay regardless. Jai wanted to call Yazmin and tell her himself what he had done but he never found the courage too. He knew by now Yazmin must have discovered he was the person who started the entire investigation against her. He was expecting some type of blow-up any day, but it never came. Yazmin's quietness worried him. What worried Jai even more is knowing that in Yazmin's investigation packet there was full evidence, in black and white on what he had done. If something like that were ever get out, it would ruin his credibility in the streets.

There was no way he could ever let that happen, ever.

Chapter 35

As Yazmin's trial got underway, she felt confident about the case. She sat stone faced at the defendant's table as she listened to prosecutors paint her as a criminal, who illegally used her job for financial gain. What they didn't know was Yazmin's attorney had already hired a private investigator to examine both transactions she had been charged with. Yazmin said a silent prayer when Attorney Shaw stood to lay out her defense. He pushed his hands into the pocket of his two thousand-dollar Italian suit and instructed everyone to turn their attention to the large projection screen on the right side of the courtroom. The courtroom was so quiet you could hear a pin drop, as he presented his case. First, her attorney pointed out the fact those exact checks were cashed at various banks, across several different states, by at least twenty different tellers. This alone proved the checks were crafted so well, it was nearly impossible to detect they were counterfeit. He continued by questioning why Yazmin was the only person charged with cashing these checks, if so many other bank tellers had done so as well. Attorney Shaw called Yazmin's co-worker Natalie to the stand, who testified that she had also unknowingly cashed a similar fraudulent check in the past. He closed out his argument by highlighting Yazmin's squeaky-clean record at her job, while over emphasizing the fact, if these transactions would have been discovered prior to these false accusations being made, the investigation process would have been handled in a more unbiased manner. "The only thing this woman did wrong, was marry the wrong man," her attorney said, pointing directly at Yazmin, before he took his seat. The jury only took one hour before reaching their verdict. Yazmin reached back and held her children's hand while she waited on the judge to read the verdict. The outburst of screams by her supporters boomed through the courtroom when the judge read the verdict, "Not guilty!"

The next morning, Yazmin enjoyed the nice breeze blowing through her car windows as she cruised down the lodge freeway. Her first stop was to the city county building, to have her concealed pistol license reinstated. After being restricted from carrying her gun the last few months while she was on trial, Yazmin was thrilled all her court dates were now over and she would finally be able to carry her gun again. With all the chaos going on in her life, Yazmin knew carrying her gun at all times was mandatory, for the sake of being able to properly defend herself at all times. Stepping off the elevator onto the second floor, she walked briskly to the small gun license room. After filling out a few forms, she took a seat and waited for her number to be called. After an hour long wait, Yazmin was disappointed to discover it would take at least three weeks before her gun license would be reinstated. A shiver went down her spine as she thought about the private calls, she had been receiving all week. Between the loss of her job and the criminal trial she had just endured, Yazmin felt as if she had put enough stress on her family, so she kept the calls to herself. Hopefully everything dies down soon, and things get back to somewhat normal in her life, she thought. Her boutique was doing extremely well, and the memberships for the social club she had just opened up were growing by the day. While Yazmin did miss the consistency of having a nine to five, she loved the freedom owning her own business gave her. As she jumped back down on the freeway headed home, Yazmin punched in the number to Bear's phone. Yazmin had hired the six foot five, bald, muscular man on the spot during his first interview for security at the club. She was aware of the jealousy and hate that came along with running a business, and her first priority would always be the safety of her and her children. "Talk to me, I'm listening," Bear's deep voice boomed over the car speakers. "Is everything all set for tonight?" she asked. Bear assured her everything was good to go. Yazmin ended the call relieved and ready to celebrate her freedom.

Chapter 36

The social club was packed from wall to wall with all Yazmin's friends and family. The celebration was in full swing with bottles, music, and food flowing throughout the club. Yazmin stood off to the side and took in the sight of everyone enjoying themselves. A single tear rolled down her cheek, as she silently thanked God for his favor during her trial. She shuddered at the thought of nearly spending the rest of her life in prison for simply loving the wrong man. She no longer had a desire to help or fix people. Terry needed her to validate him, Nadia needed her for emotional support, and Jai needed her so he wouldn't be alone. It was time Yazmin took her father's advice and worked on fixing herself before fixing other people. The crowd was getting thicker as the night continued. Yazmin glanced around the club and was relieved when she made eye contact with Bear. She was impressed at how he professionally maintained crowd control and made a mental note to increase his pay tomorrow. Yazmin looked down at the vibrating phone in her hand. It was a text message from Nadia. She smiled as she opened the message, assuming her old friend had heard about her victory in court today through social media and wanted to call and congratulate her. Yazmin's smiled instantly faded when the message finally popped up on the screen. The words, "You Only Had Him Temporarily, I Will Have Him for A Lifetime!" attached to a picture of Nadia and Jai laid out on a beach. Yazmin could tell Nadia had went out of her way to make sure she knew the photo was taken recently by the way she angled the camera, making sure to capture Jai's wrist wearing the watch Yazmin had bought him as a wedding gift. Nadia knew Jai would come back to her; he always did. In her heart, she knew if Yazmin ever changed her mind and decided to take Jai back, he would go in a heartbeat. She sent the picture in hopes of deterring Yazmin from ever wanting him again. Yazmin laughed as she deleted the message. The picture had only proved one point, divorcing Jai was the best decision Yazmin had ever made in her life. Nadia had been so busy trying to show off her and Jai's "rekindled love," she forgot to conceal her black eye. Yazmin was ready to completely close that chapter of her life, Nadia had nothing to worry about, she was done, but not before doing one last thing. Yazmin slipped into the back room of the club and opened up her Facebook app on her phone. She hit the live button and started recording. *"Hey, guys I know your girl been missing in action for a while, but I'm back now! I had to go through some shit, to really understand some shit. First let me say I'm officially single but not yet ready to mingle. (LOL) A lot of you probably know I have been fighting a case recently. What you don't know is the reason behind it. Let's just say, keep your enemies close and your loved ones even closer. I have so much to say I probably need to write a damn book. Ladies be careful out here. Just because it looks good to YOU doesn't mean it's good FOR YOU. I learned my lesson the hard way. I'm not going to go into all the details right now, just know the ones who put me last are going to feel me FIRST. Niggas pretend well, but they can only pretend for so long, the truth always come out in the end.* Yazmin held up a large envelope, while looking right into the camera. *It's time to expose some people for who they really are. Stay tuned!* Yazmin blew a kiss through the phone and ended her live. "Let them sweat for a few days," she laughed, as she sipped her drink, not knowing the danger she had just put her life in by making that video.

Chapter 37

Yazmin roughly pushed her way through the crowd, as she made her way to the loud commotion toward the front of the building. When she stepped into the lobby, Yazmin saw Bear tussling with a man. When the man's face came into full view, Yazmin had to open and shut her eyes a few times to make sure she wasn't seeing things. "Terry!" she shrieked. "Bear stop," she ordered. Bear instantly released his grip on Terry, sending him crashing to the floor. Yazmin rushed over to his side, "Terry what are you doing here?" she asked while helping him off the floor. "Don't touch me slut," he snarled, as he snatched away. Bear walked over and stood closer to Yazmin. He would snap the scrawny man's neck in two the moment he tried anything. "You didn't leave me because I'm a drunk. You left me to go spread your legs with another man, whore," he slurred. Yazmin's face flushed with embarrassment. She couldn't believe Terry was exposing their personal business in a lobby full of people. Bear began to usher everybody back into the party, trying to spare Yazmin from further embarrassment. "Terry I can explain," she calmly told him. "Your nigga already did." "He came to our house and told me everything. You were engaged before we were even divorced, bitch. Guess we all have secrets," he laughed. "Now is not the time and place Terry, if you want to sit down and talk tomorrow, that's fine, but we will not do this at my place of business," Yazmin calmly told him. "Now you care about what people think? Did you care about what people would think when you abandoned me?" Terry ranted. Yazmin tried her best to remain calm, "Terry, I didn't abandon you, I tried to get you help for years." Terry rocked back and forth. It was time Yazmin knew the truth. He flopped down in a chair, before sadly saying, "I let a grown, nasty bitch take advantage of me for years for money. For a long time, I questioned what type of man I was, until I met you." Finally, Yazmin knew the truth behind Terry's pain. It all made sense now. His refusal to experiment sexually in the bedroom, the moodiness, the anger, the severe dinking problems and the refusal to communicate. "Do you know how many times I questioned myself as a wife, as a woman, Terry? Wondering what was wrong with me? Why my husband was unattracted to me? Why my husband wouldn't talk to me? For the past two years, I have been punished by you for someone else mistakes," Yazmin screamed, becoming frustrated with the entire situation. Terry sat in the chair looking lost and defeated. "I have tried to be there for everybody in the past, now it's time I be there for myself. Goodbye Terry," Yazmin said, as she walked back into the party.

For the rest of the night, Yazmin mixed and mingled through the crowd, appreciating the love everyone was showing her. It felt good to finally be stress free, nigga free, and ready to live her best life. She had made some mistakes in the past, but she planned on using them to make her better not bitter. For a long time, she regretted leaving Terry, but after seeing him tonight she realized it was for the best. Marriages are built on love, honesty and trust, all of which they both had been broken. It was time to move on. Yazmin decided to call it a night before it got too late. The drive to her condominium was in the suburbs, where they were notorious for DUI arrests. She ignored the men fighting for her attention, as she walked through the crowd toward the door. The few pounds she had lost over the last few months from stress, had all shed in the right places. Her waist had dropped a whole size making her hips wider and her ass fatter. "Now that's a bad, bad bitch," Yazmin rapped along with Trina, while strutting out the club. "You gone boss lady?" Bear asked, while grabbing her hand, escorting her to the car. Bear had become extremely protective of Yazmin since working at the club. He could see she was a good woman had just made some bad decisions. He hoped she didn't let everything she had been through change who she was. Yazmin reached up and gave the huge man a kiss on the cheek. "Yes, I'm going home before somebody in there get me in trouble," she laughed. Yazmin jumped in her car, turned her radio all the way up, and pulled off.

Chapter 38

I Tell All My Niggas Cut the Check
Buss It Down, turn your goofy down pound
I'mma do splits on it, yes, splits on it
I'm a bad bitch, I'mma throw fits on it
I'mma bust it open, I'mma go stupid and be
a ditz on it
I don't date honey, cookie on tsunami
All my niggas like me once they get that
good punani

The Detroit Summer Anthem "Rake It Up" by Yo Gotti pumped through Yazmin's car speakers. Yazmin was feeling like a bad bitch as she turned into her Southfield condominium rapping along to her favorite song. As the music thumped through her car speakers, she rapped along with Nikki Minaj, pulling into the parking lot. Enjoying her slight buzz from the few Hennessy and Cokes she had just consumed at the social club she owned, Yazmin grabbed her purse and phone to make it in the house before the rain started to come down too hard. It was a beautiful night out for it to be mid-October, but that's Michigan for you, she thought. Just like these niggas, you never know what the fuck to expect! As Yazmin approached her front door an uneasy feeling overcame her body, giving her goosebumps. She looked around and only saw what appeared to be a disabled man scurrying to get out of the rain, he glanced back at her, smiled and continued on his way. Yazmin wondered if he received disability checks, "Rake It Up" Rake It Up" she hummed and laughed to herself. She wasn't always a cold-hearted bitch but after being in an abusive marriage for years, followed by the ultimate act of betrayal by her most recent ex-husband she was now an emotionless bitch when it came to men. Just as she put her key in the door, a shot rang out and she instantly felt a terrible burning sensation in her leg. As she looked back, Yazmin could only get a glimpse of the man she assumed was disabled a few seconds ago, holding a gun before the flash from the muzzle momentarily blinded her. Her flight or fight instincts kicked in instantly and she turned her key to get into the house. If she could just make it inside, her gun was right within arm's reach of the door. Fuck! she thought. Out of all the times to not have her gun on her! Just as she got the door open, she felt another bullet rip through her flesh. Yazmin dove in the house and kicked the door shut as bullet after bullet was shot through the door. Once she felt the third bullet pierce her body and heard the gunman on the other side of the door reloading the gun, she knew this was it. As Yazmin looked down and saw the blood pouring from her wounds, she couldn't believe her own karma had finally caught up with her. Damn, my kids, were her last thought before everything went black.

Yazmin strained her eyes against the harsh lights as she slowly opened her eyes. The beeping noise coming from the machines, sounded like loud drums. It took her a minute to realize where she was and how she had got there. "Get the nurse," she heard her son say, as he came and stood over her. The worried look on his face made her heart crumble. *I just keep putting them through bullshit*, she sadly thought. The last thing Yazmin remembered was crawling through her front door and kicking it shut. Her son filled in the blanks for her, informing her that she had actually called him and told him she had just been shot before passing out. By the time her family reached her condominium, neighbors had already notified police. In a blink of an eye Yazmin's whole life had changed. "Get the doctors, we are leaving," she instructed her son. The tone of his mother's voice told him now was not the time to question his mother's decision. Against doctor's orders, Yazmin checked herself out of the hospital. A lot of people were about to learn. Karma is a bitch but a fucked over woman is an even bigger one.

To Be Continued...

Sneak Peek
He Played Me Part 2 The Comeback

Yazmin tried to ignore the red beams that were bouncing off her body as she sat across from Max. Although he had been her drug connect for over a year, he still didn't trust her. He didn't trust anybody, that's what kept him alive for so long. Yazmin could feel Bear's discomfort as he sat next to her. She could only pray Max didn't sense it. Anything he saw as a potential weak link he eliminated. He didn't think twice about putting two bullets in the mother of his children's head when she threatened to go to the police after she caught him cheating. Max admired Yazmin from across the table. The linen suit she wore hugged her thick frame nicely. Her perky breasts were slightly spilling over the top of the lace bra she wore underneath; he was sure she had on black lace thong panties to match. Max felt his manhood rising under the table at the thought. The two had been doing business together for over a year after meeting at his assistant Chanel's birthday party. Max could tell immediately that she had not been a part of the underground world for a long time. Under her cold demeanor, there was still something sweet and innocent about her. Like anyone he does business with, he had studied her from a far before agreeing to do business with her. Yazmin was a hustler who went after what she wanted, and right now all she wanted was money and revenge.

Bio

Lisa Brown was born and raised in Detroit, Michigan. She is a divorced mother of two boys ages 23 and 21. Lisa currently has a degree in Child Development, Business and General Studies and owns She Got Style Boutique and Sitting Pretty Glam Bar, both based in the metro Detroit area. In her free time, she loves to read and travel. She hopes her writings will help to empower other women by motivating them to turn their pain into their purpose. Sometimes it takes "Losing Everything to Understand Everything," and after fighting thirteen felonies and being shot twice, she couldn't get the picture clearer.

Follow her on Facebook
https://www.facebook.com/Ms-LB-2787120948178964/
Instagram @author_ms_lb